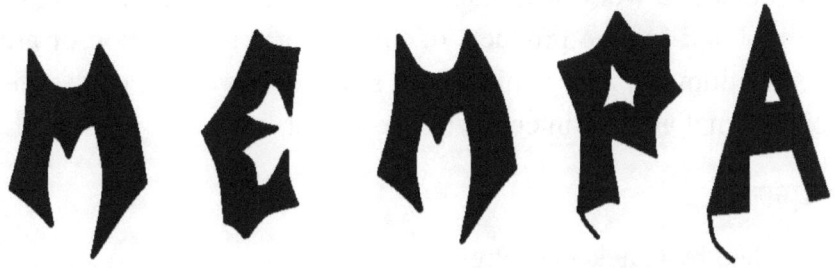

MEMPA

Nathan A. Pipkin

This book is a work of fiction. The names, characters and events in this book are the products of the author's imagination or are used fictitiously. Any similarity to real persons living or dead is coincidental and not intended by the author.

Mempa

Published by Gatekeeper Press
2167 Stringtown Rd,
Suite 109 Columbus,
OH 43123-2989
www.GatekeeperPress.com

Copyright © 2020 by Mempa

All rights reserved. Neither this book, nor any parts within it may be sold or reproduced in any form or by any electronic or mechanical means, including information storage and retrieval systems without permission in writing from the author. The only exception is by a reviewer, who may quote short excerpts in a review.

The cover design, interior formatting, typesetting, and editorial work for this book are entirely the product of the author. Gatekeeper Press did not participate in and is not responsible for any aspect of these elements.

ISBN (paperback): 9781662903106

CHAPTER

THE BEGINNING

There is a group of people looking beaten and bloody. Flames surround them with no way out. A woman screams for help, but all you can see is her mouth moving in what seems to be in slow motion. Th ere is no sound except for a ringing alarm bell. Almost everything is blurry for a second. Then something comes into focus. A bright light from nowhere comes toward your way. You hear a woman scream out, "JAAAAAMES!" as the light is getting larger and larger until… *Beep, beep, beep.* The alarm is going off.

"What the hell, turn off that damn alarm. It's been going off for the last twenty minutes," yells David, James's godfather, a middle-aged man with dark hair and eyes.

"Okay, okay, sorry," says James, a younger man of nineteen with dark hair and eyes.

Looking around in his room, James sees his clothes in a small pile on the floor. It is still dark outside, with the sun getting ready to rise soon. The apartment where he lives looks as though it might have been built in the 1960s. Some of the things are falling apart but livable. It is a small two-bedroom, one-bath place on the second floor of an apartment building. The kitchen and dining room are one with the living room, almost connected as well.

James sits up in his bed, wiping the sleep from his eyes and the sweat off his head.

As James walks out of his room, David says to him, "Another nightmare? What was this one about?"

"I'm not sure. I was holding on to a girl while the world seemed to be a blazing flame. I felt like I was really there too. I felt the heat, pain, and the girl's tears fell on me," James explains while he is walking around, getting ready.

"You know you have always had dreams that seemed very real. Just remember they're just dreams. Your just more sensitive than most," David tells James.

"Yeah, I know. I just wish I knew why my head did all this to me. Well, I got to go. I'm going to be late for work," James tells David, in a rush to get out of the door.

"Wait, wait. Don't forget your charm. You can't ever leave this behind." David jumps up and puts a necklace around James's neck.

"Damn, I hate wearing this. You have made me wear this thing for as long as I could remember knowing it makes me feel off," James says to David.

"I know, but I made a promise to keep you safe, and that's what this charm does. Trust me, please. Keep it on at all times," begs David.

"Okay, okay, dang, I will," James says with a half-smile and in a rush. James looks around and, seeing the sun will be up soon, starts jogging.

Meanwhile, on the other side of town, there is a little antique shop located on a small block in a quiet neighborhood between a few stores that are all side by side. The store doesn't look too large from the outside, but when you walk in, you have the cash register about fifteen feet on the left from the front door. Shelves line along the wall with more shelves parallel to the front window so you can see down each line for whatever you might need. The back office and storage room are five feet from the back door.

A very pretty young woman, almost nineteen, with dark hair that curls at the end and green eyes, is working hard to help her aunt by organizing the shelves. Her aunt Fran, with short blond hair and brown eyes, walks into the store to prepare for the opening when she notices the light is on.

"Mari, are you still here?" her aunt Fran calls out. "Yes, I'm in the back," Mari responds.

"Mari, I told you to go home and get some rest hours ago. Why are you still here?" Fran asks with a smile and worry in her voice. As she walks to the back of the store toward Mari, Mari's head pops out of the right side from behind the counters where she is cleaning.

"I know and I'm sorry. I was on my way out when I saw this all a mess and was trying to clean it up. While doing that I saw the shelves needed to be organized, so I started doing that and now here I am," Mari says quickly, all with a breath and a smile.

Fran looks down at the shelves and, in an almost laughing voice, says, "Mari, sweetie, thank you for this. Wow, you did a very good job. However, I need you to go home and sleep so you go finish college and get your degree. How else will you be the doctor you always wanted to be if you don't finish school?"

"I know. You're right," Mari says as she looks at her watch and sees that she only has a few hours left before her first class of the day starts. "Oh dang, I need to go now. I love you, and I'll see you later tonight." Mari kisses her aunt's cheek and rushes to get her bag and leave.

"Love you too. Be careful out there. The sun is just barely coming up," Fran says to Mari, almost shouting.

"Okay, I will," Mari responds as she rushes out the door, fixing her necklace.

As the door opens, it quickly swings into an innocent bystander. *Boom!*

Mari jumps back with her hands covering her face. "Oh my gosh, I am so sorry," Mari says while looking down at him. "Are you okay?"

"Yeah, I'm fine, but I could use some help up," James replies.

"Oh, right, sorry," says Mari as she jumps to help him to his feet.

As she gets closer to get a better grip of James's arm, their charms get intertwined. Not realizing what has happened, they naturally pull away from each other and their charms go flying.

"Oh no, my charm," they both say simultaneously.

James quickly reaches down for them and picks them both up. Not noticing that both charms almost look exactly the same, he hands her one and keeps the other.

James looks at his watch and says, "Sorry, I need to go."

James rushes off in an attempt to make it to work on time.

"What happened? Is everything okay, Mari?" Fran asks.

"I think so. As I was opening the door, I hit someone. He said he is okay and left in a hurry," Mari answers.

"Okay then, you need to get home and get ready for school," Fran tells Mari.

"I know. I'm going now," Mari says, still looking down the road she saw James run off to.

James, who is still running, gets to work just in time. It is a large factory building where they make different types of parts for car bodies out of steel and other materials.

"James, get inside. Your lucky night, kid," his boss, Mr. Thomason, a large man in size and weight with gray dark hair and dark eyes, says to him.

"Yeah, why is that?" James asks.

"The machine operator called in sick, and I need a man to operate the machine tonight, and you have been asking for that spot, right?" Mr. Thomason asks.

"Yes, sir," James answers with enthusiasm.

"Then go and get in there. Make me proud, kid," Mr. Thomason says with a smile.

"Yes, sir. On my way, sir," James says, feeling very proud. Later that day James gets home feeling lucky.

"James, how was work?" David asks.

"It was great. First, we had a call out, so I was the machine operator, then the vending machine was all messed up, so I got free food for lunch. I told my boss, and he said to enjoy. For the first time in a long time I feel like my luck has finally turned good," James says, feeling really good.

David looks over at James and says, "You look different. Come here." David starts to examine him from top to bottom.

"What are you doing, David?" James asks.

"Something is different about you. Where is your necklace?" David responds.

James lifts it from behind his shirt and responds, "Right here, why?"

David looks at the charm and in a scared voice shout, "This is not your charm. Where is yours? What happened to it?"

James stops and starts to think. "Oh, crap. On my way to work, I got hit by a door. The girl that hit me help me to my feet. Our charms got stuck and fell off. I must have mixed them up."

David looks at James with almost a dead look and shouts, "You need to go wherever that was and get your charm back. You may not come back here until you have that charm with you!" David starts pushing James out the door.

"David, what's the big deal? David, wait a second," James cries out.

David pushes James out the door and locks it behind.

"David, what the—" James yells.

"Don't come back without that charm," David yells again.

James walks back to where he ran into the girl but unsure of where the place is at. James starts to walk with what almost feels like a circle. Then out of the blue, he sees what looks to be the same place. James walks up the store and reaches out for the door when, *wham*, the door opens again on his face. James falls to the ground. Looking down at him again is the same woman.

"Not again, I'm so sorry about that. Are you okay?" Mari asks.

"Yeah, I'm okay. We really need to stop meeting like this," James replies.

Mari laughs while helping James up again.

James walks into the store with Mari. Mari walks to the back office of the store and grabs an ice pack for James.

"Here, put this on your nose. It should help with any swelling," Mari tells James as she hands the ice pack to him.

"Thanks, but I'm really okay. It's no big deal. I heal quickly," James responds.

Mari laughs like he was telling a joke.

"Oh, I have your charm. They were mixed up," James says, handing it back to her.

They look at them and see the difference.

James looks around and says, "You have a nice store here. I like the weird stuff you have."

"Thank you, my aunt owns it," Mari tells him.

Fran, who was in the back of the store, hears Mari talking to someone and proceeds to walk toward them.

"Mari, is everything okay? What happened?" Fran asks.

"Well, you know that guy I hit with the door earlier, this is him and I hit him again," Mari tells Fran with a smile.

Fran walks up front to where they are. Fran turns to put the items she is holding down on the counter next to them, seeing nothing but the back of his head.

"Who is this young—James," Fran says with shock.

"Yes, hi. Who are you?" James asks.

"Do you know each other? Where do you know him from?" Mari asks, feeling confused.

Fran looks at them with a look of fear on her face, for the day that she had prayed would never come had come.

"Mari, there is something I need to tell you, and I have not been looking forward to doing so. First, I do know James from a long time ago. You and him were—" Fran starts to explain when a sudden loud sound of glass breaking comes from the back room.

"What was that?" James asks.

"Not sure. Stay here," Fran tells James and Mari. Fran walks to the back of the store slowly.

As she approaches the back, James and Mari stand up, watching her movements like they expect her to say, "Just the wind."

Fran turns the corner and walks through the doorway and says, "Something broke the window."

At that moment James and Mari exhale with relief. Suddenly, Fran is thrown across the store like a tornado had thrown her. James and Mari quickly rush to help Fran. Fran looks at them and yells, "RUN NOW!" Fran puts her hand toward James and Mari palm out as Mari is screaming, "NO."

In a blink of an eye James and Mari are outside the store. They run to the doors to open them, but the doors appear to be completely locked in place. All they can hear is things being broken and screams on the inside.

"We need to go!" James tells Mari.

"NO, I'm not going without my aunt. She is all I have. I can't leave her," Mari tells James while still trying to open the doors.

"I don't know what happened or how we got out here. What

I do know is that she can handle herself with whatever she did to us," James says to Mari.

"What are we supposed to do now? Where do I go?" Mari asks James.

"Come with me to my place. If your aunt knows me, I'm sure my godfather knows you," James tells Mari.

Mari looks at the store one more time with tears in her eyes. "Okay, let's go," Mari replies.

James and Mari walk to James's apartment building. As they start getting closer to the apartment, James looks at his door and sees that his door is open. As they get closer, he notices his door is not just open, it has been broken into.

"Wait here, I need to make sure it's safe," James whispers to Mari. James walks in to his home and looks around, not missing a single spot. His entire home has been destroyed, much like Fran's store. James falls to his knees after not seeing any sign of David around.

Mari walks into the apartment slowly, looking at James on his knees. She wants to say something to help comfort him, but having the same thing happen to her only but an hour ago, nothing comes to mind. Mari puts her hand on his shoulder, hoping to bring some kind of peace. James looks at his room and notices that his dresser is still in the same spot it always is, like it has never been touched.

James stands up and walks to the dresser. Everything looks normal. He tries to slide it just a squeak with no luck.

"Mari, can you please help me?" James asks.

Mari walks over and tries to help James move the dresser, yet still no luck.

"Wamit," James yells.

Mari looks at him like, "What was that?"

James look back at her and says, "David always said it. Like saying damn but nicer."

Mari smiles at him. James starts walking away from the dresser when Mari bumps into the dresser and a small squeaky sound can be heard. James turns back quickly and pushes the dresser to the side.

"What…how…huh?" James says with confusion.

James looks at the back of the dresser, and there appears to be a little handle at the bottom. "What is this?" He grabs and pulls it up. Almost like rolling down, it lifts without any problem. At that moment James is looking at stuff that looks hundreds of years old in what looks like a walk-in closet. "Mari, can you please hand me that duffle bag over there?"

Mari grabs the duffle bag. "How much do you think will fit in this bag?" Mari asks.

"Not sure, but I'm going to put as much as I can," James responds.

"Where are we going now?" Mari asks.

"I have an idea. Follow me," James responds.

James and Mari walk down to the parking garage. He walks up to a car with a cover. James grabs the cover and in one strong lift and pull reveals a 1969 Cadillac completely restored.

"If you have this, why do you walk everywhere?" Mari asks with curiosity.

They are getting into the car and ready to leave.

"I lost my driver's license a few months ago," James answers.

Mari looks at James and asks, "For what?"

James puts the car into drive and says with a smile, "Speeding." They peel out of the parking place on their way to their next location.

James and Mari arrive at a large building that looks like a warehouse.

"What is this place?" Mari asks.

"This is where I work. We have a shower, food, water, and

a break room where we can figure everything out," James tells Mari.

They walk up to the building in what looks to be a completely deserted parking lot. James walks to the door and attempts to pull it open without luck. He steps back, and the door opens with Mr. Thomason, James's boss, standing there.

"James, what are you doing here?" Mr. Thomason asks.

"We have had a very long day and need somewhere to go," James tells Mr. Thomason.

"Come on in," says Mr. Thomason.

"Where is everyone? This place should be full right now," James asks Mr. Thomason.

"I gave them the time off," Mr. Thomason says with a smile.

All three walk into building and head straight to the break room. As they are making their way to the break room, Mari is looking around at the place, all the different machines they use and how they have a hot metal just sitting on the side not being worked in any way. They walk through, going around the machines. Other than the melted metal, everything seems to have been off for some time. They walk into a room that looks as though it could be the start of a motel lobby. Mari sits down at one of the tables as James gets Mari some coffee while he is telling Mr. Thomason some of the events that has been happening.

"So, you're telling me that between her aunt's shop being destroyed, your home being destroyed with all this, you have no clue what is happening?" Mr. Thomason says to James.

"Yes, that's what has been going on. Not sure who to go to for help," James tells Mr. Thomason.

"James, can I see your charm? I think I can help," says Mr. Thomason.

"Mr. Thomason, I never said anything about my charm," James says with confusion in his voice.

Mr. Thomason looks at James and Mari with a dark smile and says, "OOPS, you caught me."

At that moment Mr. Thomason grabs James by the throat, pinning him on the wall, lifting James at least a foot off the ground with only a single hand.

Mari screams, "NO!"

In fear she grabs a chair from the nearest table and starts hitting Mr. Thomason across the back, hoping he will break his hold on James. With a single swing of his free left arm, Mr. Thomason hits Mari, sending her flying across the room like she is a rolled-up piece of paper. Mari hits the ground hard, the fear of death on her mind.

"Give me what I want, and you will live. Your charm and hers and it will be like this never even happened," Mr. Thomason tells James.

"Why are you doing this? What did I ever do to you?" James asks.

His face is red, and he is running out of air.

"It's not you, dear boy. This has nothing to do with you. I just want the charms you both have, and I'll let you live. Then everything can be just as it was in your little pathetic lives," Mr. Thomason says to James as his voice turns eviler by the second.

Mari lifts her head and body as if trying to do a push up. Mari looks at James, and at that moment she lifts her right hand up, palm out, and in a very strong voice shouts, "FREEZE."

In less than a second Mr. Thomason looks at her and turns into a frozen demoncile.

Mari runs to James, who is still pinned on the wall, and tries to make the now-frozen hand of Mr. Thomason open. She picks up the chair she had hit him with and hits him again. This time she shatters the demoncile into what could be called shaved ice.

"What was that?" James asks Mari.

"I do not know. I have never done that before. I just felt it, and it came out," Mari tells James.

They look at each other for a split second and almost jump into each other's arm.

"Are you okay?"

"I think so."

James and Mari ask at the same time.

"I thought it was supposed to be safe here," Mari tells James while smacking him on the arm.

"AAAWW, I don't know who is good and bad! I'm sorry," James responds.

They both take a look around to make sure that nobody is around. After James and Mari feel everything is safe and locked, they go back to the break room where they were originally.

A few hours later Mari turns to James and asks, "You said there was a shower here, right?"

"Yeah, here let me show you," James answers. He takes Mari down the hall toward the shower.

In this room there are seven showers, seven toilets, seven sinks, wall of lockers, and a big cupboard full of clean towels.

"Hate to ask, but are there any different clothes I might be able to change into?" Mari asks, shy like.

James walks over to one of the lockers that has no lock on it. "See if any of these fit. This lady left her stuff here," James tells Mari.

"Are you sure?" Mari asks.

"Oh yeah, she hasn't been here in a month. She brought these and never came to get them," James tells Mari with a smile.

Mari grabs a towel and turns on the water. James starts to walk out of the room.

"Please do not leave, I'm scared," Mari begs James.

"Okay, I'll sit over here then," James says to Mari.

James sits down in a chair that is close to Mari. He hears her starting to take off her clothes and grabs one of the towels, draping it over his head to make sure nothing is seen out of respect for her. Mari steps into the shower, and everything turns quiet, nothing except the sound of the shower.

A few minutes into the shower and James decides to break the silence with a comment.

"Talk about a crazy day, huh?"

"Yes, you can definitely say that," Mari responds.

"Sorry, I don't like silence that much," James tells Mari.

"I can tell," Mari says.

"Where did you grow up?" James asks.

"Around here," Mari answers. "You?"

"Same," James responds. "How old are you?" "Almost nineteen," Mari responds. "You?" "Nineteen," James replies.

Mari starts to turn off the shower. "Can you please hand me a towel, James?" Mari asks.

James grabs a towel, turns his body around, and puts it on his left shoulder. "Here you go," James says.

Mari grabs the towel and looks through the curtain and sees that James has his back turned toward her for privacy. As Mari steps out of the shower, she looks over at James and watches him put the same towel back on his head like a few minutes ago.

Mari finishes up getting dressed, and she walks up to James and asks, "Do you want to shower as well?"

"Yeah, I was just waiting for you so I know you're, I mean, we are, safe," James responds.

"Okay, good. Your turn," Mari tells him. Mari puts the towel on her head as James steps into the shower.

"AAWW," James screams in a high pitch.

"What's wrong? Are you okay?" Mari asks, worried.

"Sorry, yeah, the floor is cold. Do you always take this cold of a shower?" James asks.

"Hush your mouth, and stop being a sissy," Mari says to James while laughing.

James starts to laugh as well. Then he turns on the hot water, and the room starts to get very streamed up.

"Wow, that is hot. I'm stepping into the hall," Mari tells James.

"Okay," James replies as he enjoys his hot shower.

James steps out of the shower, covering himself quickly.

"Mari, I'm finished," James announces but got no response from Mari. "Mari, you there?" James asks louder.

There is still no response. James rushes to his clothes and quickly gets dressed. He picks up a wrench lying on a nearby table. He starts walking back to the first room slowly, just in case. He gets to the room, still calling out for Mari, and sees her sitting on the couch passed out peacefully. James slowly puts down the wrench on a table, trying not to wake Mari. James goes to the couch and sits next to her, placing his jacket over her. She turns in her sleep and lies on his shoulder. Mari starts to shiver, and James does the one thing he knows what to do. James slowly takes a deep breath and starts to release body heat almost as if he is exhaling through his body, warming up them both.

A few hours later a big loud boom wakes them both.

"What was that?" Mari asks with her heart pounding.

James jumps up off the couch to go look.

"Wait here," James tells Mari.

"Not a chance after last night," Mari says to him.

James picks up the wrench from the table and starts walking toward the front of the building. They both hear footsteps coming closer and closer. James and Mari put their back along a wall, blocking themselves from being seen. The footsteps are only a few feet away when James is about to jump out.

Then a voice calls out, "James, you here?"

James turns the corner, almost hitting his friend with a wrench. "James, what's up, man? No need for the wrench," AJ, a guy with black hair and green eyes, says while catching the wrench before getting hit by it.

"AJ, thank god, it's you," James says with relief.

"Who is this? Can we trust him?" Mari asks.

"Yeah, he's my best friend," James says.

"Plus, I'm one of the good guys," AJ tells Mari.

All three of them walk to the break room and see the demoncile that is still all over the floor. AJ looks down and starts to speak when James cuts him off.

"We have had a very long night. First…" James starts to explain.

"Your charms got mixed up, and when you went to switch back, your aunt's store got attacked. Then you went back home, finding your place destroyed. Then came here and found out that our boss 'Mr. Thomason' is evil, and I bet that those are his remains all over the floor. Now we are here. Does that about cover it all?" AJ asks.

"Yeah, how the hell did you know all that? Why am I not feeling worried about it?" James asks.

"James, I am your guardian. I have been here with you this long to keep you safe. Plus, you and I are connected. That's why you know you can trust me," AJ tell James and Mari.

"If you are his guardian, then where have you been this whole time?" Mari asks in a rage.

"Mari, I know and I'm sorry. I wanted to be here, but I had to wait," AJ explains.

"Wait for what?" James asks.

"Wait to see if you could do what you did. Now that you now know, I can fill in the rest," AJ tells them. AJ starts walking to the front of the building.

"Where are you going now?" Mari asks.

"Oh, I'm not. We are. Please follow me."

The three of them walk to the parking lot. James and Mari

look around, and even though things look the same, somehow it all looks so different.

James looks around and asks, "Where is my car?"

AJ looks at James and says, "Where we are going you don't need your car. However, knowing you would ask that, I made sure it is safe and sound where we are going."

"Okay, cool. Where are we going?" James asks, feeling confused.

"We are going somewhere safe, where you don't have to worry ever again," AJ tells them in a peaceful way. "Please take my hand.

This is a ride you have never had before."

James and Mari walk up to each side of AJ and take a hand. At that very second the world seems to change right before their eyes, like watching a movie move from right under their feet.

CHAPTER

A NEW BEGINNING

James wakes up from the same type of dream he always has. He looks around, and it looks like nothing has changed. James is in his room, on his bed. He sits up on the side of the bed confused, trying to figure out if it was all just a dream.

I know that was no dream. That was too crazy, James thinks. He stands up and gets dressed.

James opens the door like any other day and says, "David, I had this crazy..."

James realizes that he is no longer at home but in a whole new place. It looks like a paradise of some kind. All the people are peaceful looking. No yelling, fighting, or any kind of hate. Open smiles and happiness. Little kids are playing in what looked to be a dirt road. The homes look like they were all just built, but they were not the largest. Everything is just so simple and beautiful.

James looks around, unsure of where he is and with no memory of how he got there. He starts walking and looking around at everything. *This place is too perfect. Where the heck am I?* James thinks.

"You, my friend, are at your new home. The most peaceful place you will ever see," AJ responds.

"I said that in my head. How did you hear me?" James asks.

"Well, like I told you before, we are connected," AJ tells James while giving him a hug.

James looks around, even more in disbelief of how beautiful the place really is.

"So where are we exactly?" James asks.

"Somewhere in the Hawaii Islands between Lana'i and Kaho'olawe, under a protection bubble. That way no one know we are here, and we can keep our people safe," AJ tells.

"Where is Mari? Is she okay?" James asks, worried.

"Oh yeah, she's fine," AJ answers.

"Where is she at?" James asks.

"Over by the lake. Down this hill a little. She's been going there for the last six days," AJ tells James.

"Oh, okay…SIX DAYS! I was out for six days!" James says in fear.

"Yeah, well, some people when they come here for the first time can't really handle the trip so they pass out. You happen to pass out for a very long time, but we made sure you were okay," says AJ.

"Can I see Mari?" James asks.

"Oh yeah, go back the way you came. Go down the hill, and you should run into her," AJ explains.

James starts to walk the same way he came. He comes to the hill that is maybe fifteen feet and within minutes found himself at a lake with the clearest water, the greenest trees, and a beautiful field of grass. James slowly walks up to a very large tree that stands maybe fifteen feet from the water, and there he sees a beautiful woman sitting with a book in her hand. She was leaning back on the tree in a way that looked so comfortable, as if where she was lying was made just for her body. She lifts her head out of the book, looking toward the water, and turns her head. James quickly realizes the woman he has been staring at for the last few minutes as he was walking up is, in fact, Mari. Her mind hasn't seen him yet. James looks at her smiling, happy to know how safe she really is.

Mari notices James walking toward her and jumps up from her place as if something had bit her and runs to him, wrapping her arms completely around his neck.

"Oh my gosh, you are alive," Mari says to James with excitement.

"Yeah, I just woke up and found AJ. He told me you were over here," James replies.

"When we got here, you looked around for a second and dropped. You scared me so bad. I was checking on you every day," Mari tells James.

"Thank you for that. I feel a bit lost with everything going on though. Like, why is all this happening?" James asks. James is standing there looking at Mari, feeling happier than ever.

AJ gets a message to bring Mari and James to the Main Building. AJ walks to them, seeing how happy they are.

"I hate to do this to you, guys. We got called. I need to show you guys something. Come on, I need you to come with me," AJ tells Mari and James.

"We will talk later," Mari says to James.

"Where are we going?" James asks AJ.

"Something has just come to my attention, and we are going to it," AJ responds.

All three of them start walking up a road that James has not realized he had walked not that long ago. They pass a lot of homes and other places. James can't believe all this is in a place nobody even knows about. Then they walk up to a large building that looks like it must be at least three hundred years old.

"What is this place?" James asks.

"This is the Main Building. Anything and everything come through here. This is like our city hall," AJ tells him.

They walk to the front of it, opening a large door that must be half the size of the front wall. James and Mari walk into the building full of nerves with AJ leading the way. There is a long hallway with doors on each side. It almost looked like a school with the way the halls and classrooms are set up. In the hall there are glass cupboards all the way down the hall.

As they walk through the building, James and Mari are looking around at all the artifacts that have been collected over time. Almost like walking through a museum, they are looking at everything with amazement, pointing at things, saying things like, "Look at this." Then they turn a corner to the right to another hallway.

AJ finally comes to a set of double doors at the end of the hallway and tells both Mari and James, "Through here is something special just for you."

AJ pulls on both doors, and at that moment Mari sees her

aunt Fran and James sees his godfather David. They both quickly run to them, squeezing each other so hard none of them could barely breathe.

As AJ stands to the side watching the family reunite, he knows that they need to find out what they can do. AJ gives them like five minutes, then tells Mari and James, "I hate to do this, but it's time to see what you can do."

"Wait, how is this possible? We saw you get attacked. And, David, you were nowhere to be found. Is this real, or are you just trying to help your side? I'm feeling so lost I don't know what to do," James says in a panic.

"It's all real. Your family has been a part of all this for centuries," AJ says to James with a smile. AJ walks up to James and puts his fingers on his temple.

James's facial expressions go from scared to relax almost instantly.

"Feel better now?" AJ asks.

James nods his head to say yes.

All five walk into a room that is more battle-training ready.

"Okay, let see what you two can do. Mari, will you please join me first," AJ says.

Mari steps forward.

"Can you tell me what you did or felt when you froze Mr. Thomason?" AJ asks Mari.

"Well, I guess you can say I was scared and really wanted him to stop hurting James. I put my hand up like this, palm out, and he froze," Mari explains.

"Do you think you could do it again right now?" AJ asks.

"I have no idea," Mari responds.

Mari stands out from the others and tries to freeze a little target. She closes her eyes, slowly puts her right hand up, palm out, and at that moment Mari opens her eyes.

At that same moment AJ is making a suit of armor come to

life. As Mari is concentrating on her task, AJ is about to have the suit armor attack her aunt. Mari hears her aunt scream and turns around and sees the suit of armor attacking. In that split-second Mari's hand jumps in front of her, and the suit freezes at a blink of an eye.

Fran watches as Mari uses her gift and smiles with tears in her eyes. "I thought you were really scared. You faked it," Mari says with anger.

"I'm sorry, I just had to help you unlock what you did," Fran explains.

Mari looks around and thinks about what just happened. Then she realizes that it did help. "Okay, I forgive you. Just please do not scare me like that again," Mari asks.

"Okay, I promise," Fran says to Mari, giving her a hug for the fear she had to endure.

James looks at AJ and asks, "What can I do? I have never done anything like that."

"I am your guardian, which means I know everything about you. I have never seen much from you, and I don't know why," AJ tells James.

"If I don't have anything special about me, then why am I here?" James says in frustration.

"You are here because you belong here. You just need to unlock your gift. We can all do something. We all can do spells. However, your special gift, you need to find it. No one's guardian knows what it is until it gets unlocked," AJ tells James.

"Well then, how do I unlock it?" James asks.

"It could be stress, fear, anything. That's the problem. No one really knows. I'm really sorry to say," AJ tells James.

James looks around at everyone in the room. "Tell you what, take me back where I was. Because if that's the case, I don't need to be here," James tells AJ.

"Give me time to help you, and if you are not happy after

two days, I will take you anywhere you want to go," AJ says to James.

James walks out of the room and starts to head outside. James doesn't know why he is even here. He feels like he is just wasting everyone's time.

James is almost at the exit, and Mari runs to catch up to him.

"James, James, please wait for a second," Mari shouts.

James opens the exit and holds the door for Mari.

"I just wanted to tell you we will figure out what your gift is," Mari says to James.

"I don't know, I need to think," James says to Mari. James starts to walk away when AJ runs up to them, out of breath.

"Hey, guys, I was just asked to take care of a little business, if you would like to come along," AJ says, hoping to get James to help.

"What is the job?" Mari asks.

"There is creature on the loose that we need catch," AJ explains.

"How bad is it?" Mari asks.

"It destroys anything and don't care if you are good or evil," AJ tells them.

"What is it?" Mari asks. "It called a Jaggle," AJ says.

"What the hell is that!" James asks.

"A creature that looks like half eagle, half jaguar. It is faster, much larger, with no remorse for anything," AJ explains.

"I don't know if that is a good idea," James says to them.

"I say let's do it," Mari says with excitement.

"Go, have a good time," James says to Mari.

"No, you're coming too. I want to know you have my back," Mari says to James with a sturdy voice. Mari is looking at James straight in his eyes.

"Okay, fine. I'll go, I'll go," James says to Mari. Mari smiles, and James starts to as well.

AJ looks at both of them and says, "Okay, let's go."

"Is there anything we need before we go?" James asks.

"Nope, we have everything we need," AJ tells him.

AJ takes both of their hand, and in a blink of an eye, the world changes in front of them again.

Mari looks at James, who is bending down like he is feeling sick to his stomach.

"James, are you okay?" Mari asks as she rushes to him.

"Yeah, I'm okay. That's crazy how everything is melting away like that. I need to get used to that," James says, trying to breathe.

"Yeah, it can be rough. Try doing it sometime. Anything happens to anyone. You could land somewhere like the top of a volcano, and everyone is gone. It's not that easy," AJ says, kind of laughing.

James sits up and realizes they are all standing on some kind of a monument with a walkway of stairs.

Looking at a city and a grass field on the side of the walkway, James asks, "Where are we?"

"Not sure what city this is. Just keep a lookout," AJ tells him.

From where they are standing, you can see most of the place. Cars are parked along the side of the road where the grass fields are. There are large buildings that look as though they might be places of business or even homes.

"Well, hurry up, James, because I think I see the Jaggle now," AJ says.

All three of them look straight ahead, and there they see a creature the size of a large rig with two trailers. This creature is running around like a dog in a yard playing around.

"HOLY CRAP! That's a Jaggle," James says to AJ.

"Oh yeah, we are lucky. That's a baby," AJ says in response.

Mari and James look at each other with shock and awe.

"I'm just joking, but that one is not full grown," AJ says with a smile.

"That is not helpful," Mari states while giving him a dirty look. They start to walk toward the Jaggle.

"How do we stop that or catch it? It's so huge, and we are so small," James says.

"I'm hoping that Mari can freeze it, and you could help me transport it," AJ answers.

James starts to feel like he is useless. "I'll be here if you need me," James says to them.

"Are you sure?" Mari asks.

"Yeah, that way you guys can do what you need to do," James replies.

AJ and Mari start walking ahead and start planning how they are going to stop the Jaggle. James is standing back watching them. As AJ and Mari get closer, James notices that the Jaggle is getting very close. James is getting more and more nervous watching the Jaggle getting closer by the second, but it doesn't look like AJ or Mari knows where it's at. They are looking around like they hear it but see nothing. The Jaggle turns away from them. James breathes out hard. Then the Jaggle turns like it is being called by someone.

James continues to look on. Then in seconds he watches Mari and AJ get slammed into the ground by the Jaggle who just busted through a large building. With his heart stopping for a second, he blinks and sees that Mari and AJ are still standing there.

James, unsure of what is going on, screams, "MOVE AWAY FROM THERE!" Neither Mari nor AJ hears him.

James starts running as fast as he can to get to them, still screaming out, "MOVE NOW!"

AJ turns and feels all that is about to happen. AJ tries to help Mari by pulling her to the side, but the Jaggle slams through the building between them. Mari is getting hit more than AJ. James runs even faster to get to her and help. AJ, knowing James is coming to help, goes after the Jaggle. James slides down and lifts up Mari into his arms while sitting in the middle of the street. Full of anger and fear, James holds Mari close in his arms. James does not notice that the Jaggle is three hundred yards behind him as he tries to make sure Mari is still alive. The Jaggle is standing there looking at James and Mari, ready to attack. The Jaggle bends its head down ready to move. Then it jumps up and runs toward James and Mari.

The Jaggle is getting closer and closer by the second, flipping cars and anything that's in its way. James looks behind him with Mari still in his arm, and he sees the Jaggle coming. Unable to move without the possibility of Mari being safe at the same time, James starts to panic, letting all his emotions go into a large scream like exhaling without a sound.

At that same moment the Jaggle is a second away from James

with its mouth wide open ready to eat them both. A large stream of fire bursts out of James and incinerates the Jaggle in seconds. AJ looks on at James lighting the Jaggle on fire with his body. The Jaggle drops down, burning into ash and blowing away into the wind.

"How did you do that? That was incredible," AJ asks.

"I don't know. I never have before," James responds.

"Did we win?" Mari asks.

"Mari, are you okay?" James asks.

"Yes, I think so. What happened?" Mari asks.

"I'll tell you later," James responds.

AJ helps Mari get to her feet. James stands up, dusting himself off. AJ is still looking at James in shock.

"What?" James asks.

"That really was incredible," AJ says to James.

AJ takes their hands, bringing them back to their new home. Mari, with a few cuts and bruises, is being helped by James. Fran and David walk up to see how the job went.

"What happened? Mari, are you okay?" Fran asks with concern.

"I am okay, Aunt Fran. I got caught in the cross fire, but thanks to James we are safe," Mari says with a smile.

"What do you mean James?" Fran asks.

"James found his gift—or in this case, gifts—are," AJ says with pride.

"Really, wow! What can you do? Why did you say gifts?" Fran asks.

"Well, he can—" AJ starts to say.

"I saw the attack before it happened, and I was able to burn the Jaggle," James says.

"What do you mean, burn the Jaggle," David asks.

"I don't know, I got upset, and this stream of fire came out of me.

The crazy part is I was holding Mari and she didn't get burned at all," James tells them.

Then a lady walks up behind them and says, "You are a firestarter, but not just any kind. You're the strongest one ever known.

Congratulations on that, but please be very careful not to be careless." James and Mari look at the lady and ask as she is walking away, "Who was that?"

"That is the person who controls everything around here. She is serious and very caring. Her name is Estrella Damkin, aka the Bright Star, or Star. To address her, call her Miss Star," AJ tells them.

Later that night James and Mari are getting out of the medical room.

"I cannot believe they were able to heal me that fast," Mari says in shock.

"I know. You're not even going to have a scar," James says to her.

They are both walking down the road, looking around at the beauty that surrounds them.

"How is this so real?" James asks.

"I have learned to enjoy things as they happen. You never know how long they will last," Mari tells him.

"I hate to say this, but in my experiences, nothing ever stays good too long," James tells her.

"Think about it like this. I am here, and nothing is going to change that," Mari tells him with a sweet smile.

They are looking deep into each other's eyes when they see something red fly by.

"What the heck was that?" James asks.

"That was Phoebe," answers Miss Star, a middle-aged woman with dirty-blond hair and brownish-green eyes.

Mari and James jump backward as Miss Star appears out of

nowhere. "Where did you…how did you…?" James asks in complete shock.

"I think you underestimate what we can do here. That's okay," Miss Star says with a smile.

"I'm sorry, I didn't mean to say," James quickly starts to apologize.

"James, it's okay. You're fine," Miss Star says.

"What did you mean about 'That's Phoebe'?" James asks.

"That was Phoebe, who is a phoenix," Miss Star says.

"Wow, that's incredible," James says to Miss Star with excitement.

Miss Star at that moment turns to walk away, then suddenly turns into a ball of light like a star, and flies away. James and Mari both watch as she flies above the crowd.

"Wow, that was something else," James says with a smile on his face.

Mari looks at James and asks, "What do you think? Are you going to stay around now?"

James looks at her and says, "I think I might be able to find a reason to." James walks her down the road to her home.

"This is me," Mari tells him.

"Okay, are you sure you're okay?" James asks.

"Yes, I am fine. Thank you for walking me home," Mari says, playing with her hair.

"I'll see you tomorrow," James says to her, walking away.

Mari walks into her home, closing the door behind her.

CHAPTER

A NEW SIGHT

The next morning James and Mari walk down to the eating area, an area that looks like a very large picnic table that fits everyone who lives in their community. Above the table is a cover that is designed like a tent but is made out of magic-enforced aluminum.

"Mari, where are we going?" James asks.

"I am taken you to where we all eat," Mari replies.

"Don't we all eat in our own homes?" James asks.

"Sometime, but there are days during the week when we all

get together and feast like one big family. Miss Star like it like that," Mari explains with a smile.

As they approach the eating area, James notices that everyone is there, including Miss Star with her phoenix.

"Does Miss Star always have her bird with her?" James asks.

"Yes, she needs to. Phoebe is still young," Mari answers.

"What do you mean, still young? How do you know that?" James asks.

"Watch them for a minute," Mari replies.

James and Mari sit down at the table seven chairs down from Miss Star and Phoebe. James is watching as Miss Star is eating and Phoebe the phoenix is walking on the table, pecking at the plate Miss Star had put out.

Miss Star looks at Phoebe and asks, "Phoebe, please eat right. Stop acting like an animal."

At that moment Phoebe jumps into the air with her wings completely open over the chair next to Miss Star, and in a single jump like motion, Phoebe turns into a young girl with white-reddish mix hair and gray eyes, no more than nine years of age. James is struck, looking at her in disbelief.

"James, it is not nice to stare," Mari whispers to him.

"Sorry, that was just, wow," James says, still with shock and awe on his face. "So how does this work? We just grab what we want?"

"Yes, that is the way it always works," Mari tells him.

James looks around at all the food on the table, having trouble deciding what to eat. James notices that his favorite breakfast food, French toast, is not that far from him. He reaches for it when someone else grabs the last pieces before he can. James sits back and says, "Aw, man."

Mari looks at him, asking, "What's wrong?"

"I found my favorite, and someone got the last piece," James tells her.

"Get close to it, and wait for a minute," Mari tells James.

James stands next to the tray that was holding the French toast, looking around. Not sure what is going to happen, James looks for someone to bring it. Then the tray fills back up. James smiles, grabbing most of the tray. James sits back down next to Mari, telling her, "That was so cool. I love this place."

A short time later AJ walks up to James at the table.

"Hey, bud, are you ready?" AJ asks.

"For what?" James replies, trying to swallow his last bite of food.

"Training. After what you did yesterday, we need to know you can control your gift," AJ replies.

"When do you want to start?" James asks.

"Right now," AJ replies.

James and Mari get out of their chairs, following AJ to the same place where Mari was being trained prior.

"Okay, James, are you ready? What happened when you were out there? How did you start that fire stream," AJ starts by asking?

"I saw the Jaggle running toward me, and I was so scared that I let everything I had go," James answers.

"What do you mean, let everything go?" AJ asks.

"I have always been able to warm up a little with a heated exhale, if you would. Instead of going through my mouth, it would come out through my skin. I did that but with all of my feeling. The fear, anger, everything, and let it all out. The result was what you saw," James explains.

"Okay, let see if we can do it again, but this time with control," AJ says to James. At the same time AJ slams his hand together and says, "Shiem."

Then a shield starts to cover the entire room.

"What is that for?" James asks.

"That is just in case you don't burn anything. Miss Star would kill us if anything happened to this place. It has been around since before her," AJ explains.

"Better safe than sorry, I guess. Let's have some fun," James says to AJ.

AJ tries to throw things at him to put a little fear or anything into him, but nothing is happening. AJ uses different way to try motivating him to release, yet still nothing.

AJ and James are training for hours, and James is having a hard time getting anything to work right. They are trying different ways to make James scared and happy, trying to focus on whatever gets him to feel the same way he did when he was trying to save Mari but without having any luck. The most James can get to come out is a little heat off his body that is making the heat in the room rise from a cool 68 degrees to 120 degrees in seconds, moving the temperature up and down.

"Okay, I don't know what to do. It is getting hot in here, and all we seem to do is raise the temperature," James says with frustration. James is sitting along the wall to take a break.

AJ looks at him and says, "Try meditating. Put yourself back to that place you were."

James starts to think about the way he felt on the mission when he released the fire from within him. For James it is almost like he is living that moment all over again. This time he was in control, not having anyone tell him what to do but to be more natural about it. He is looking back watching as Mari and AJ almost die all over again; the way he was holding Mari in his arms as the Jaggle starts running toward him; the fear of losing Mari, a person he really doesn't know but feels like he has always known, scaring him to the point of just wanting her safe no matter what.

As James is thinking about this, AJ is walking back over to him from getting a drink and notices James starting to stream up.

AJ takes a couple of steps back knowing what's about to happen. James is deep in thought, remembering the event, and his eyes turn almost a solid black; and at that moment a soundless scream comes out of James, much like before, and a stream a fire comes out again. AJ is watching this stream. The stream almost looks like it is looking for something, causing harm. Then AJ yells out, "James! I need you to come back to me! James!"

Then, just like watching the event play in reverse, everything goes back to the way it is.

James is still sitting there but with tears in his eyes.

AJ runs up to check on him. "Are you okay? What happened?" AJ asks.

"I started thinking about that day when I first made the fire. Then it was like I was there again," James says to AJ, scared.

"I can tell you that you lit up again. The stream looked like it was looking for something. I think it was your fear trying to stop what you were scared of," AJ tells James to help ease his mind.

"Did it hurt anything or anyone?" James asks.

"No, that's the thing, it wasn't trying to. It was just protecting you, and because you were safe, it just looked and stayed in place.", AJ tells James.

"Okay, good. I have never felt like that before," James tells AJ as AJ helps him to his feet.

"I can imagine that was new for the both of us. You are doing great though. Just relax and I think we should be fine," AJ tells James. James stands up, feeling upset in a way he never has.

AJ looks at James with a smile and says, "Look on the bright side, we figured out how to unlock it."

James walks out of the room, pushing through AJ. AJ, seeing how much this is hurting James on the inside, tries to apologize to him for what he had said.

James, still looking upset, tells him, "I don't like this feeling of pain." James keeps walking down the hallway to the exit.

"I completely understand that, I'm sorry. We only need to know how it works so no one gets hurt," AJ tells him.

AJ and James walk outside to see that they have been in training almost all day.

Mari walks up to them, asking, "How did it go? Did you do anything good?"

"That's all on your perspective," James says as he walks away. "What happened in there?" Mari asks AJ.

"James unlocked the fire, and now he is very scared that he might hurt someone," AJ tells Mari.

"Is there anything we can do to help?" Mari asks.

"No, all we can do is keep him calm. Now that it has been unlocked, I don't know what can help him," AJ says to Mari.

Mari starts to think about what AJ just said. She rushes to catch up to James. "I heard about the training. Are you okay?" Mari asks James, but he just keeps walking, paying no attention to her.

"James, please talk to me. I want to help in any way I can." Mari is hoping to get James to open up to her.

Suddenly, James stops and looks at her. "Do you know what opened me up? Remembering you almost dying. Reliving that moment again. That moment scared the hell out of me. I don't want to think about it. Leave me alone, I don't want to feel that way again," James tells Mari with tears in his eyes.

James starts to walk away, then turns back toward her. "The part that pains me the most was thinking about you getting hurt again. I don't know why, but I can't lose you or feel like I'm losing you again. It hurts too damn much." James then turns again and walks away.

Later that night James is in bed asleep having a nightmare. He is moving around in fear. He can't control what is happening, only watching. The world is burning while he is holding a girl. She never really had a face until now. She looks just like Mari. He starts to get scared, and he is very upset. He is seeing everyone at this place that he has just met calling out his name, like they are trying to get to him, but he is pulling further away, completely out of reach.

AJ and Mari pop up at James's home, feeling something is not right. At the same moment Mari and AJ come to James's room and see him struggling in his sleep.

Mari looks at AJ and asks, "What is happening?"

AJ looks at Mari and says, "He is having a really bad nightmare. We need to wake him up."

AJ and Mari each takes a side of the bed in an attempt to wake James up.

AJ puts his hand on James's head, trying to get through to him, maybe get him out of the dream. James's skin is very hot, burning AJ. Then a stream of fire starts to rise out of James like his fear is being carried out to the conscious world. Mari puts her hand on James's chest right above his heart. Her hand starts to get colder as James is heating up more, matching opposite temperatures perfectly until the fire dies down. AJ stands up and backs away, watching Mari take control over the fire stream.

James jumps awake from his nightmare, looking at Mari and AJ.

"What happened? Did I hurt anyone?"

"No. Thanks to Mari, I don't think you will either," AJ says with a smile.

"What happened?" James asks.

"Well, you had a nightmare, and we felt something was wrong, so we came to check on you. We saw you were getting hot, and Mari put her hand on you to try cooling you off. It worked, and now we are here," AJ explains.

"What were you dreaming about?" Mari asks.

"It's just a reoccurring dream I have had for a long time," James tells them.

"If it is that bad to where you catch on fire, I would talk to someone about it," Mari tells him.

The next day James gets called to Miss Star's office, which is located in the same building as the rooms where Mari and he had been reunited with their family and where the training room is. James is walking down the hallway feeling nervous. Unsure where her office is, James starts looking around until he sees a little door on the side close to the wall about the size of a mail slot but as tall as a door. On the slot is the name "Miss Star." James steps back to see if he can find a full-size door but nothing can be found. He knocks on the wall above the slot, hoping a door will pop up somewhere.

"Who is it?" Miss Star asks.

"It's James. I was told you wanted to see me," James replies.

"Okay, stay there. Don't move," Miss Star says.

James, unsure what is about to happen, steps back and looks side to side, waiting for Miss Star to open a door. Then like a suction tube James slides through the slot, and then he is standing in front of Miss Star in her office. He looks around her office. The office looks like a building all on its own. There are walls full of bookshelves and her own twist in her design like a dean at a university with artifact from only god knows when on her desk and some also along the walls.

James, feeling confused, looks at Miss Star, asking, "What? How?" "Magic," Miss Star answers. "Now, from my understanding, you have unlocked your gifts but it pains you to do so. Can you tell me what is the pain you are feeling?"

"I don't know how to explain it. My mind is sad, feeling like I'm hurting someone. I'm angry but not sure at what. I'm scared, but like scared that someone might get hurt from this," James tells Miss Star.

"You are one of the most powerful firestarters I have ever felt. Most firestarters enjoy doing it and love the pain. You, however, don't enjoy it at all. I have something that belongs to you," Miss Star says to James while pulling his necklace from her desk drawer.

"How did you get this?" James asks while jumping to his necklace.

"I have my ways," Miss Star says to him.

"I think you should put this on until we can make sure you know how to control your gift," Miss Star requests.

"I think that would be a good idea, ma'am," James says as he puts it on.

"You may go back to whatever you might to do," Miss Star tells James.

"Okay, thank you, but how do I get out of here?" James asks.

Miss Star snaps her fingers, and like nothing happened, James is back in the hallway.

James walks away from the slot wearing the necklace that Miss Star had given back him. Feeling the same way as he did before, although not as tied down as he did before, James lifts the charm, looking at it, unsure of the feeling. After seeing everything is the same, he doesn't think twice about it.

Then Mari walks in the hallway, shouting, "James! There you are.

I've been looking for you. How did the meeting go?"

"I think it went well. Miss Star gave me this back," James says to Mari, holding the charm.

Mari looks with a smile. "Is that to make sure you do not burn anything down?" she asks in a whisper. "I think so," James replies, also in a whisper, and smiles. They both walk outside.

The next day Mari is walking home from the lake where she was meditating and realizes that it was getting dark. Mari, feeling good, walks into her home.

Then Fran, David, AJ, and James shout, "Surprise."

Mari, covering her face with her hands, is very shocked but

with tears and smiles. One by one they each walk up to her, wishing her a happy birthday. The look on Mari's face almost says that she forgot about her own birthday. She thanks each person, and they all sit for dinner with Fran telling stories about Mari when she was little. Mari is blushing with embarrassment but is loving everything that is happening.

By the end of the night, James is in the kitchen taking care of all the dishes.

Mari walks in, telling him, "You know you do not have to do that."

James looks back and smiles at her, replying, "No, I do. This is your birthday. Your aunt was nice enough to make all this. The least I can do is clean up to say thank you."

Mari gives James a look with her hair pulled to the side and smiles.

James can feel everything what is on her mind. James smiles back, looking Mari in her eyes, and tells her, "I agree, but not yet."

Mari looks back at him like he just heard what she had just thought.

James just says, "No, I didn't hear any thoughts. I could just tell by your look what was on your mind."

Mari smiles again and asks, "If you think you know, then why not?"

"To be honest, I'm not sure. It feels like there might be something else coming soon. Just want to make sure you know before," James tells her.

Mari looks at James with confusion.

James takes her hands and says, "Trust me."

Fran and David walk in with Fran asking, "Everything okay?" Mari blinks and turns her head, saying, "Yes, everything is fine."

"We need to get home," David tells James.

James nods his head, giving Mari a hug and doing the same to Fran, thanking her for dinner.

James and David leave.

Fran asks Mari, "You sure everything is okay?"

"Oh, yes. Everything is just fine, I promise," Mari says, walking by Fran, giving her a kiss on the cheek as she goes to bed.

A few weeks have passed, and James is living like everything is normal. He and Mari have been training with other forms of magic, learning all the little things that can help them, without extreme results. Life has turned almost normal in a sense.

James is sitting with David for dinner when David says, "You have been so happy. What have you been doing?"

"I feel happier. AJ has been working with us. For the first time I feel like I belong," James replies.

"Have you been getting hot at all?" David asks.

"Ever since Miss Star gave me this charm back, I haven't been worried about anything. Not even feeling hot," James tells David. David looks at James with a smile.

James looks at his watch and says, "I'm sorry, David, I got to go."

"What do you mean you got to go? Where are you going?" David asks.

"I'm supposed to meet Mari and AJ at the library. AJ wants to continue training with the books," James tells David.

David looks at James curiously and says, "Get out of here. I know you're not going to do anything dumb around here."

James shows up to the library in a hurry. "Sorry, I'm late. David had a dinner set up for us," James explains.

"Not to worry about it. You made it, that's what matters," Mari says, hugging James.

"Are you ready to see what we have to offer as far as knowledge?" AJ asks.

"Let's do it," James replies.

They walk into the building with James and Mari looking

around. From the outside the building looks like it might be a medium-size two-bedroom house. From where they were standing, they could see that they were at the top of what looked to be at least twenty-five stories. The library looked almost like a giant spring shape. The more you walked through it, the deeper you went into it.

They proceed to walk through the library to where AJ said would be a fun place to start. Around halfway down AJ starts showing them books on mythical creatures that really exist. James, being excited, starts walking further through the library, looking around. James starts looking for a book that he feels like he needs to find although he has no idea what the book is. James stops suddenly and pulls a book out. He opens the book to read about a child born of pure good and evil that will burn the world.

"James! There you are," AJ says, touching James's shoulder. James jumps back, not realizing AJ is there.

"Are you okay? We have been looking for you for a while," Mari asks him.

"Yeah, sorry. I'm fine. I was looking at the books, and I found this one," James tells them.

"Why way down here? Did you know what you were looking for?" AJ asks.

"No, I wasn't looking for it, but wait, what you mean down here?" James asks, looking at the middle, seeing he is almost all the way down at the end of the library.

"What is this book?" AJ asks.

"I'm not sure, but it was saying something about a child that would burn the world," James replies, handing the book to AJ.

AJ opens the book, looking at it. "Where did it say that at? It looks like a basic history book," AJ says to James.

James looks at the book again, and it looks normal. Nothing like what he just saw. James, feeling confused, grabs the book and rushes out of the library straight to Miss Star's office.

James, rushing to Miss Star's office, runs to the slot on the wall and knocks hard, shouting, "Miss Star, Miss Star, I need your help."

Before James can knock again, he finds himself in Miss Star's office. James rushes to her desk, but nobody is in the office. He looks around, trying to figure out how he got in if she didn't let him in. Then out of nowhere a light flew in through the slot, and Miss Star appears, standing there, looking at James.

"James, how may I help you?" asks Miss Star.

"I'm sorry for popping up like this, but I was in the library, and I found this book," James tells Miss Star, handing it to her.

She looks at the book, opening, closing, and moving the pages around. "It looks like a basic history book," Miss Star tells him.

"That's what AJ said too, but when I first grabbed it, it was saying something a child burning the world," James tells Miss Star.

Miss Star looks at James, seeing that what he speaks is the truth. Miss Star places the book on her desk and tells James, "I don't know what you think you saw, but it is clearly just a normal book. Could you have maybe saw something else, like you saw the Jaggle kills AJ and Mari, then when you blinked everything was still okay?" "I guess that is possible," James says, calming down.

"I think that might have been what happened," Miss Star says to James. She walks him out, then pops up back in the hallway. Miss Star sits at her desk and moves the book closer. She runs her hand down the spine and opens the book. She sees that this book is the prophecy book that was taken a long time ago, however it has been disguised as another book.

Who did this, and why did James find it? What does this all mean?

CHAPTER

THE KEEPER

A few months have passed, and James has been perfecting all the magic he can do. However, he still thinks about that day he found the book in the library and cannot understand what happened. He remembers what it said about the child burning down the world but no one else could see it, then it was gone like it was never there. Could he really be seeing a prediction? Every time he goes to the library with his friends and is reading every book, he is hoping to find the one that has the prediction in it but with no luck. All the while he is making it seem like he wants to learn everything he can to sharpen his skills.

Then one day he gets a message asking him and his friends to come see Miss Star at her office. James, praying for an answer about the book, jumps at the opportunity to go see Miss Star.

"James, are you okay? You seem a bit excited about this meeting," Mari asks.

"Yeah, I'm fi ne, just want to see what Miss Star has to say," James replies, rushing to get to the office. James knocks on the walls as always and shouts, "Miss Star, it's James, AJ, and Mari." *Boom!* They are standing in front of her desk.

"Hello to you all, I hope your day has been pleasant," Miss Star greets them.

"Yes, good so far," AJ and Mari reply.

"I have a job for you all. I have been hearing that you have been studying a lot and working on your crafts. I need people who I can trust and that I know can do the job. Plus, I really like you all," Miss Star tells them.

James, feeling like this is something really big, starts to worry about the next thing that is being said.

"We have a creature on the loose that needs to be stopped quickly.

However, this will not be easy," Miss Star tells them.

"Yes, ma'am, what is it?" AJ asks.

James quickly turns his head to AJ with a confused look.

"You will be stopping a Pure Keeper," Miss Star says to them.

"Excuse me, but what is that?" Mari asks.

"A Pure Keeper is a creature that can influence anyone of purity to do the most sinful things, such as anything that is sinful from stealing to killing. One touch and if you're pure, you are under its spell," James says.

"Very good, James, I am highly impressed," Miss Star says to James.

James smiles and says, "Thank you, Miss Star. How do we stop something like that? It's almost demon like, and there is no known way to stop it."

"You will need to kill it," Miss Star says.

"Okay, can I just set it on fire like with the Jaggle?" James asks.

"No, you need to get a drop of blood from two of the victims and put them in the Keeper's mouth. That is the only way to stop it. The Keeper cannot intake the infected blood. It only feeds on the actions, then kills the victims. Oh, the victim must be alive and cannot have sinned yet. They must be pure of heart still, which means infected but have not lost their soul. Please stay safe," Miss Star says to them as they pop back into the hallway.

"Are you happy now that you know what Miss Star wanted," AJ asks James.

"That's not what I was praying for, but let's get to work," James says to AJ.

"How dangerous is this Pure Keeper?" Mari asks.

"Very, if you're still a virgin," AJ says to Mari.

"Seriously! That is what you meant by pure," Mari says to them loudly.

"Yeah, there is nothing purer. That's why it's called the Pure Keeper. It feeds out all the sins they do, killing the purity," James tells her.

"Why are you so worried? Not like you're a—" AJ says to Mari as her face turns red.

"AJ, that's none of your business. Whether she is or not is on her," James says, stepping in the way.

"Thank you, James," Mari says, smiling at James.

"Knowing this, I think you should stay here for your safety," James says to Mari.

"There is no way I am staying here. You guys need my help. We are better as a team," Mari tells them.

"Okay, fine, but for your sake, I hope nothing happens," AJ replies. Then AJ puts his hand up, and they all show up to a quiet little town in the middle of Southern California.

They find themselves in a small abandoned one-room house. There are a few things left like a chair with a spring sticking out, a couch that is missing the cushions, a bed in a room that looks like nobody has touched it in years. The walls have holes throughout.

"What are we doing here?" James asks AJ.

"This job is going to take some time, so we need a place to stay until we are done," AJ responds.

James starts looking around. "How long will we be here?" James asks.

"Until the job is done. When the Keeper is dead, we are out of here. I don't like being in a place like this either."

"How do we do this? It is not like we can walk through the town asking if anyone has ever seen a creature that is having people do bad things," Mari says to AJ.

"No, but we do walk around look for something that's not quite right and go from there," AJ replies.

The three of them walk out through the door in a pursuit to find the Keeper.

After a few hours walking around, Mari starts feeling like there is no hope of finding anything. She sits down in frustration, making it seem like she is very tired.

"I need a break," Mari says as she sits down on a bench a few feet away from her.

"Yeah, I need to sit down as well," James says.

AJ looks at them both and thinks that it's good idea. They sit on the bench.

"What are we looking for?" Mari asks.

"That's the hard part, not really sure. Something just pops out, and then we go from there," AJ responds.

James is looking around, watching what people are doing. Things look so normal. Mother walking across the street with a stroller, kids playing in the grass—everything is completely normal. There is a little store across the street where a few kids park their racer scooters outside and run inside. Moments later they run out with candy in their hands. Looking at this makes James smile.

Then he notices and girl around seventeen or eighteen years old with blond hair and blue eyes. She looks a little off—hood over her head, face looks dark, like she is about to do something bad. She doesn't even look at anything or anyone. She is walking like she is on a mission. Then like it's an everyday thing, she walks in, shoots the clerk, and walks out of the store like everything is okay.

James jumps up and says, "What about that?"

"What happened?" Mari asks.

James looks up, and nobody is there. James, with a look of confusion on his face, is unsure of what happened or what to do. James starts looking around, hoping to find who he just saw.

AJ looks at Mari and says, "James just had a vision. What did you see, James?"

"Her walking into the store, shooting the clerk," James says, feeling relief.

They make their way to the girl, and AJ bumps into her to see if she has a gun. AJ finds it and hands it to James, who throws it in the sewer drain in the gutter. AJ apologizes for bumping into her.

The girl walks into the store and reaches for her gun but quickly finds out that nothing is there. She panics and runs out of the store.

They watch what she does and start to follow her to see where she goes. Maybe this is who they are looking for.

The girl is taking them through alleys and backyards. They follow her to an empty warehouse. This place looks like it might have been a warehouse that could have been a mechanic's garage at one point. The walls and roof have aluminum paneling. There is a second-story walkway for maintenance that is around the whole building and connects to the middle of the building. There are some windows in the framework. Most of them are broken.

They look inside, and it looks like a place where runaways get to be free.

Then a man walks out from a room and starts talking to the girl. AJ sneaks around the other side to hear more. The man asks the girl if she did what she needed to do. She tells him no; she lost the gun. She tells him she's sorry.

The man says, "It's okay. Here, try again," as he hands her another gun. He tells her to get it done if she wants to feel free again. She walks away, and the man walks back into the room where he came from.

AJ gets closer and finds a window to the room. The man passes by a mirror, and AJ sees that the man is their creature in disguise. AJ quickly rushes back to James and Mari.

"We need to get out of here and get that girl," AJ says in a rush.

"Why, what's happening?" James asks.

"That guy she was talking to is the creature. She is going to try and shoot the clerk again, and we need to stop her and get a drop of her blood," AJ tells James.

They all move fast to try and stop the girl.

James runs up to catch up with AJ and asks, "How do you know that she's going to try again right now?"

"That thing gave her a gun and told her to try again, that killing him will set her free," AJ replies.

"So, what do we do when we catch up to her? She'll just find another way. We can't stop her every time?" James says to AJ.

They all stop where they are standing.

AJ looks at James and says, "You're right. We need to take

her back to where we are staying at until we stop it." "I am not kidnapping anyone," Mari says.

"Not kidnapping, just making sure she doesn't condemn herself before we get what we need," AJ says to them.

They start walking back where they think the girl will be.

On their way to get to the girl, they see a group of sixteen-to seventeen-year-old boys walking next to train tracks. One of the boys looks over in the woods one hundred feet from them and sees his brother and calls for him.

"I haven't seen you for a while. Where have you been?" the boy says with a smile.

The other boy just keeps walking.

"Hey, what's up, bro. What is your problem?" the boy yells at his brother.

Then a train starts coming through, and the other boy turns to his brother.

"Hey, are you okay?" the boy asks.

The other boy starts walking to his brother. With his arms open, the boy welcomes his brother, until he notices that his brother looks like he is about to hurt him.

"Bro, what are you doing? What's wrong?" the boys ask. The train is getting closer.

Mari can tell what is about to happen and screams out, "Run, get away from him."

All the boys look at her, unsure of what she means. Then the other boy grabs his brother by the neck and lifts him off the ground. Mari and James start running to help. Then, as the train is about to pass, the boy throws his brother in front of the train, killing him. Mari screams and freezes the boy but was a second too late.

With nothing more they can do; AJ tells them they need to try and stop the girl.

They catch up to the girl walking into the store. They rush

to stop her before she can shoot the clerk. They walk inside and move slow so as not to startle the girl.

The clerk, with gray hair and blue eyes, looks at the girl and says, "Hey, Tammy, you're back. Are you okay? Your mother and I have been worried about you lately. Where have you been?"

"Dad, please don't," Tammy says to her father, Mr. Smith.

"What's wrong? What are you doing?" Mr. Smith asks.

"It's the only way to stop the pain. It's the only way to stop the pain," Tammy starts repeating.

"What pain? What are you talking about?" Mr. Smith asks.

Tammy reaches behind her back for the gun. Mari walks up to her, grabbing the barrel of the gun, freezing it with her hand.

"I'm sorry to jump interrupt, but do you carry gun here?" Mari says to Mr. Smith.

"Yes, miss, right here," Mr. Smith answers.

Mari steps forward when Tammy says to Mari, "Excuse me!"

Mari turns around and says, "I know what you're about to do, and you do not need to do this, Tammy."

"Tammy, do you know? Think, girl. What are you about to do?" Mr. Smith asks.

"No, I don't. I know I'm tired of this," Tammy says as she lifts the gun to shoot her father. Tammy pulls the trigger once, twice, three time, but nothing happens. "What is wrong with this thing?" Tammy screams out.

"Hard to fire when completely frozen."

Tammy tries to run when AJ puts his hand on her and says, "Doze." Tammy falls into AJ arms. He carries her out of the store. Mr. Smith looks at them, taking Tammy, but before he could ask, Mari tells him,

"Do not worry. We will help her. She will be back to normal soon, I promise."

Mari gets outside and rushes down the street back to where

they are staying. Mari gets back to the house just in time to watch AJ ties Tammy to a bed.

Mari walks up to AJ and asks, "How long will she be out?"

"Maybe a day or two," AJ responds.

They walk out of the room into the living room when Mari asks, "Where is James?"

"I thought he was with you," AJ responds.

"No, I have not seen him since the store. I thought he ran by your side," Mari tells AJ.

"Okay, give me a minute to find out," AJ says, closing his eyes. AJ starts to see what happened.

James was stepping outside the store to make sure that nobody comes in and get caught in any cross fire when some guy walked up to him asking if everything is okay.

James looked at him and said, "Yes, everything is okay."

The guy put his hand on James shoulder and said, "You should come with me."

James left with him.

"Wait a minute, I know that guy!" AJ says with fear.

"Who is it?" Mari asks, scared.

"That's not a who, that's the Pure Keeper. He has James." AJ rushes out the door with Mari right behind him.

They both head straight to the warehouse where they saw Tammy went to. They walk around the side to see if James is inside or not. They see a lot of people inside who all look like Tammy did. They walk around back to try and see if there is anything that might be able to help them get more into these kids. They find an extremely large dumpster like what you would find at a construction site. AJ climbs up to look inside, then Mari follows him.

AJ looks back at Mari and says, "You might not want to see this."

Mari looks over the top and says, "Oh my," while trying not to scream.

They find that most of the dumpster is filled with bodies. Then two kids come from the top balcony of the warehouse and toss two more bodies over the side into the dumpster like nothing. Mari starts to panic about the heartless action.

AJ looks at Mari and tells her, "Mari, I need you to keep it together for me. This is disgusting and wrong, but remember this is what we need to stop, okay?"

Mari nods her head. "Okay, okay, you're right."

"James need us as well," AJ says.

"You're right," Mari says.

They hear the Keeper start talking to someone. AJ and Mari look closer through the window and see that the Keeper is talking to James.

The Keeper is telling James that all the pain he feels will be gone, all he needs to do is kill one person he cares for. He knows what all the pain is—the feeling of being alone, the feeling that nobody understands what he is going through, feeling completely trapped in his own head. Then the Keeper asks James if there is any weapon he would like to use. James tells him he already has one and takes off his necklace.

Mari kicks in the door. "That is enough of that," Mari says.

"Perfect timing. Now we don't need to look for you," the Keeper says to Mari.

"James, I know you're in there. Look at me," Mari cries out.

"Oh, he is here, but not the way you want him to be," the Keeper says to Mari.

AJ comes from behind and pushes James out of the way. Mari puts her hand out and screams, "FREEZE."

The Keeper turns to ice, then breaks free in seconds. "That was cute, but you can't hurt me with your little tricks," the Keeper tells Mari.

Mari stands back in fear.

"My turn," the Keeper says.

The Keeper looks at James and says, "James, don't you have something you want to do?"

James looks at Mari, and a large stream of fire starts rising from his body. James throws his hand forward, and the stream runs straight through Mari.

AJ screams out, "NO!"

After a few seconds, James pulls back and puts the fire stream out. Mari stands up, surprised she is still alive. AJ is looking as surprised as she is.

"Well, that didn't work the way I thought. Let's try this," the Keeper says to Mari.

The door swings open, and there is Tammy holding a new gun straight at Mari. Mari, frozen in fear, calls out for James to help her. Tammy walks around Mari and AJ to stand next to the Keeper.

"Take her out, Tammy," the Keeper tells Tammy.

Tammy is holding the gun straight at Mari when James grabs the gun from Tammy and says, "No, she is my kill."

Tammy looks at James and says, "I was told to do it." Tammy tries to grab the gun from James, but James hits her with a right hook, busting her lip open.

James takes the gun and points it at Mari and says with a smile, "Sorry."

James quickly turns and hits the Keeper in the mouth with the same right hook.

"What do you think you're doing?", the Keeper asks while wiping his face.

"I know the only way to kill you is with the blood of your victims. I was under your spell until my guardian hit and cut my knuckle, breaking the spell, giving my mind back temporarily, just enough time to know what I was doing. I hit Tammy with the same hand that got cut and now you are dying," James says to the keeper.

The Keeper is on the floor screaming out, "What? NO! You can't do this to me. Nobody can stop me."

"I guess I can," James says with a smile.

The Keeper starts to fall apart, turning into a pile of blackish-blue slime and ooze. All the kids start to get their mind back. Tammy looks over at the pile of Keeper and moves fast to the side.

James puts his hand out, helping Tammy up, asking, "Are you okay?"

"Yeah, I think so," Tammy says to James.

"I'm sorry I hit you. I would never do anything like that normally," James tells her.

AJ, James, and Mari gather everyone still alive up and walk them out of the building.

Mari looks at James and asks, "If you knew what you were doing, why did you try to kill me with fire?"

"To be honest, I knew that my fire would never be able to hurt you. Not really sure how I know that, but something tells me you are the only one who can never get hurt from it," James tells Mari.

Mari gets a look on her face that's curious. She tries to understand what James meant but doesn't ask.

The three of them are walking back to pack up their stuff when James asks AJ, "How did you get my mind to come back to me?"

"Do you remember when I told you the bond between a guardian and their witch is strong," AJ asks.

"Yeah, I remember something about that," James replies.

"Well, the Keeper has never done against anyone like us, let alone got one us under a spell. So, I used our bond to break his. I was hoping it would work," AJ tells James.

"Glad it did. Wait, you didn't know if it would for sure?" James says with shock.

"Guys, let's go home," Mari says to them.

They stand side by side and pop back home.

AJ looks at Mari, and James and tells them, "I know we lost someone today, but please remember that was nobody's fault. Things happen sometimes. We do our best to save who we can. I'm proud of you, guys."

James looks at Mari and says to AJ, "We might have won against the Keeper, but we lost that kid. That will never be a win in any book."

Mari nods her head, agreeing.

"I know, I was just trying to help. Sorry," AJ says to them.

The three of them part ways to get some sleep. James can't help but feel like something is about to happen. He puts his necklace back on and goes into his home.

CHAPTER

THE BREACH

Bright and early James finds himself awake wondering what he is feeling. He gets out of bed and gets ready for the day. He goes outside and walks down to the lake. James sits by the tree where he first saw Mari at his first day on the island. James thinks about everything that has happened while he has been here, how things have turned in his favor but left him feeling more lost, unable to figure out why this started when he got here. Then he thinks about the book he found and how he can't find any book that says anything about it anywhere in the library. Th at might have been the book he needed. Miss Star had to be lying about it so he would not ask so many questions. Th ere had to be a spell on it or something. If there was a way to get into her office without her knowing, he knows he could find that book.

"James, hello," AJ yells, standing in front of him, waving his hand. James looks up at AJ and says, "Oh, hey, sorry."

"You good, bro?" AJ asks.

"Yeah, just been doing some thinking," James replies.

"I know what is on your mind, and you need be careful with that. I'm not the only one who can read your thoughts," AJ tells James quietly.

They start walking toward the breakfast tables. James looks at Miss Star and sees that Phoebe has grown, almost looking twelve years old now. Miss Star looks back at James and smiles with a hello nod.

James is taking a bite of food when a very loud alarm goes off. All the young look around like, "What is happening?" Miss Star and all the elders stand quickly. Miss Star tells all elders to get the young to somewhere safe.

James and AJ run to Miss Star and ask, "What's going on?"

"That is the intruder alarm. Someone or something is here that shouldn't be," Miss Star tells them.

James looks around and asks, "Is there anything we can do?"

Miss Star looks at him and tells him, "Find Mari and help us protect our home."

James nods, and he and AJ rush to find Mari.

Mari, who woke up late, is awakened by the alarm. She tries to get dressed in a rush, unsure of what is happening. The sound is so loud she can't hear as she calls out for her aunt. She walks out of her home when James and AJ run up to her.

"What is going on, guys? What is that sound?" Mari asks, holding her ears.

"We will tell you on the way," AJ tells Mari, rushing her to help.

The alarm turns off, and they head to the Main Building. They walk up to the Main Building, and everything seems quiet. Cautiously, the three of them walk into the Main Building, looking around at every corner. Slowly opening up the front door, they walk down the hallway, checking every room. They come across Miss Star's office. The door slot is the size of a normal door, and its hinges are broken. James peeks inside and finds two guys tearing up the office.

The three of the steps into the office, and AJ says to the men, "Last I checked this is not your office. Maybe I can help you find something."

The guys, both wearing clothes that look ripped from fighting, turn, looking to three teenagers standing in front of them.

One of the guys says, "Yeah, we are looking for a book, old and has…"

The other guy smacks him, saying, "SHUT UP! We are not supposed to say anything."

The first guy says, "Oh yeah, I forgot."

James looks at them and says, "I know you guys are not that stupid." "We are not stupid, just a little slow," the first guy says.

"Shut up you idiot," the guy says, smacking the first guy again.

"There is no need for any violence. Everyone can walk away from here," James says to them.

"We need you guys to leave, if you would be so kind," Mari says to the two guys.

"Okay, well, I guess so since you asked so nicely," the second guy says, starting to walk between AJ and James out of the room. Then he turns to hit them with a spell.

Mari sees it coming and casts her own, screaming, "Freeze."

He turns into a solid icicle. The second guy looks at him, grabs his hand, and disappears from the room.

James turns his head toward the bookshelf; and right in front of him, a foot away, is the book. James thinks it would so easy but not like this. *We need to stop these guys first.* He turns to the door back on the wall to check around the corner and sees more people running down the hallway. James looks at Mari and asks, "Can you freeze the floor?"

"I have no idea," Mari says, shrugging her shoulders.

James looks at Mari and says, "Try, I'll try to distract them."

James jumps out to get their attention. Before he can say anything, he gets hit in the head with some kind of a spell. The only thing heard by anyone was the word "Kount." James flies back, hitting the wall and roof, leaving him knocked out on the floor.

Mari screams out, "Jaaames!"

James, in the last second of consciousness, looks up and one of the men running back looks down at him with a look like he knows him before disappearing. Mari and AJ run to James. They rush him to get medical help. It appears that James is the only one who is badly hurt.

Everyone else only has some cuts and bruises.

James can see what happening around, but his eyes are closed. His body is completely knockout; however, he can hear and see everything around him. Mari, AJ, David, and Fran are sitting by his bed side just in case he wakes up.

Mari, more so than anyone, feels guilty for him jumping out when he did. Mari keeps replaying that moment over and over, trying to figure out what she did wrong. The last words he said were, "I'll distract them," then the way he hit the wall and roof, then dropped. Mari is spending most her time crying about it.

Mari falls asleep, and James hears Miss Star by the door. She is asking about James's condition. The doctor tells her that James took a very hard hit and they are worried about his brain. Miss Star asks why no magic treatment is working.

The doctor, a woman with dark hair in a bun and glasses, says, "The magic was strong and dark. A simple spell somehow amplified in a way I never seen. Plus, when James hit the wall, his spine and neck was hit hard."

Miss Star seems very upset about the whole thing.

"Are you okay?" the doctor asks Miss Star.

"Yes, I am just worried about what I might have done. Not just like I sent him out, but well, you know," Miss Star tells the doctor. They both walk away.

After a few days in the bed, one night, Mari is left with James. She takes his hand and starts to pray.

> *"I am not sure what you think of people like me who can do what I do, but God, can you please help my friend. Whether you think we are bad people or you love us, I still love you. I have not prayed for a long time. I know what ever happens to me is your choice. To be honest, I really do not know what to say. I feel like this is all my fault. I promise to stay as true to you as I can. I do not have many friends. God, please save James."*

Mari has tears running down her face and is all over James's hand.

The next morning James starts to move around. James is having a dream about someone coming to him.

"James, this is not your time," a lady tells him.

"Who are you?" James asks.

"Give me your hand," the lady tells him.

James, feeling safe and calm, puts his hand out. The lady takes his hand. James starts feeling warmth all over his body, with all pain disappearing.

Mari, who was sleeping with her head on his bed, lifts her head up to see James moving. Mari calls out for AJ.

AJ rushes into the room. AJ starts calling for the doctor, saying, "I need the doctor in here. He is waking up."

The doctor runs into the room with James still moving around but not awake yet.

The lady smiles at James, telling him, "Go back now, you have much more to do."

James's eyes pop open in a panic like he had been fighting to wake up the whole time.

"James, I'm a doctor and you are in the medical facility. Can you hear me?" the doctor asks.

"Yes, I can hear you?" James responds.

"Can you tell me the last thing you remembered?" the doctor asks.

"Which part?" James asks.

"Let's try before the accident," the doctor says.

"I remember everything, including hitting the wall," James tells the doctor.

The doctor looks at his eye and says, "I'm shocked, you look like nothing ever happened."

"Is that a good thing?" James asks.

"It's always good when an injury like this has no issues," the doctor tells him.

James tries to sit up when the doctor tells him, "You need to slow down. You need to rest."

"How long have I been here?" James asks.

Mari says, "Three days."

James starts to slide out of the bed, saying, "I have rested."

Then out of nowhere a ball of light flies into the room, and

Miss Star appears, saying, "James, you need to stay in bed for now. We need to do more test, and if everything looks good, you can leave tomorrow, I promise."

James sits back and says, "Okay, I'll stay for one more night, but you need to tell me about that book."

Miss Star face turns shocked, and she says, "Okay."

Mari has a look of shock on her face and asks, "Should I leave?"

"Yes, that might be best," Miss Star says to Mari.

Mari starts walking out, looking at James with confusion.

Miss Star closes the door to the room. "First, let me start with, you are not crazy. Far from it," Miss Star tells him.

"What do you mean?" James asks.

"That book you speak of and found is a book that many people have been looking for a long time. Someone had put it there and disguised it to look the way it did," Miss Star tells James.

"So, what I saw was what I saw. Why did it look different when I closed it?" James asks.

"When you grabbed it, your hand went down the spine and that is what stops the spell until closed again," Miss Star tells him.

"Okay, so why are you telling me this now?" James asks.

"When you were in my office, you saw the book and did go after it. You decided to stop what was going on. That told me protecting our home means more. This is my thank you," Miss Star tells James.

"Can you please tell me what I was reading?" James asks.

"What you were reading was a prophecy about a child borne of pure good and pure evil that shall burn the world as it stands to separate the two," Miss Star tells James.

"Why did the book call me to it?" James asks.

"That I don't know. You might be drawn to strong magic," Miss Star tells him.

"Why me though? Who am I?" James asks.

"I'm still trying to figure that out," Miss Star tells him.
"Do we know who the prophecy is about?" James asks.
Miss Star tells the story.

"The only child that I know of whom was born of good and evil was lost in a war that happened long time ago. The mother was of pure good family and the father was part of a pure evil family. It was said that they left their families to be together and away from the war. The man fell in love with a girl, and they were married, and she was pregnant. Then one night she went out to get firewood for their home when she found him with his family. Before she could say anything, she had caught him killing an innocent, which he had never done before and claimed he never wanted to. He was good from an evil family until he killed. That made him evil. Before he could return home, she left him and went back to her family. After giving birth to the child, her family felt the child would be a risk because of his bloodline. Then one night a war broke out and she needed to get her baby to safety and sent the baby and a friend out to sea until everything died out. She was watching the boat drift out it when it was blown up, and her child and friend were never found,"

"Did anyone went looking in the ocean?" James asks.
"Yes, but like I said, nobody was ever found," Miss Star explains. James sits back in awe.
"That is why I'm trying to figure out why everything is happening," Miss Star tells James.
"Who were the guys that were here? How did they even find or get in here"? James asks.
"Not sure who they were, but they want something we have.

Nothing has been reported missing yet," Miss Star tells James. "Do you have any more questions"?

"No, but before they got away, there was a man who ran past me and when my name was said, he looked at me like he knew me," James tells Miss Star.

"Are you sure?" Miss Star asks.

"Yes, I'm very sure. That was the last thing I saw before being here," James tells Miss Star.

"Thanks for telling me. Now please get some rest," Miss Star tells James.

Miss Star walks over to the door and opens it. Mari is standing there, waiting, when Miss Star tells her she can come back in. Mari walks in and sits next to James.

"Is everything okay?" Mari asks.

"Yeah, is now. I'm starting to understand more," James says to Mari.

The next day James gets home to have David telling him to rest. "I don't need rest. I need to find out who that was that broke in our place," James tells David.

"You don't need to worry about it. Everyone else is working on it as we speak," David explains to James.

"I just want to know if this place is so safe. How did anyone get in here?" James asks.

David turns his head with a look like he knows something.

"What is it?" James asks.

David looks at James and says, "There is a way, but it doesn't normally happen."

"What is it?" James asks.

"The group that hit us is the group known as the Spawn of Evil or SE. They have been after us from a long time. Most of them are family. Only a person of good can get through the shield, but they can be bringing others through with them. That's why we don't know how they get through," David tells James.

"What do you mean?" James asks.

"See, with this group, to be a member you need to kill an innocent and that puts a mark on the back of your neck, which makes you a member," David tells James while thinking about it.

"What are you not telling me?" James asks.

"Nothing I'm just thinking about this. I need to talk to someone. I'll be back," David tells James while rushing out the door.

The next day James is trying to understand what is happening, so he walks down to the library. As he walks down the street, people are asking him how he is feeling and thanking him for everything he did to help and letting him know that if there is anything, he might need to let them know. James, unsure what to say, just thanks them all. James walks into the library and walks to the front counter asking the librarian for help in finding some info.

A lady with dark hair and wearing glasses turns around, asking, "What can I help you with, young sir?"

"Yes, miss, I need to find out what I can about different people or groups in the world," James asks, trying to be subtle.

"I need a little more than that. There is a lot of groups out there. Just so you know, my name is Rae. I hate being called miss," Rae tells James.

"Sorry about that," James apologizes.

"You didn't know, but you do now. Don't let it happen again," Rae says, joking with a smile.

"I need to find info on SE," James tells Rae in a whisper.

"SE, huh? Is that a code word for something?" Rae whispers back.

"Sorry, I'm looking for Spaw—" James starts to say, still in a whisper.

"I know who you're talking about. I was messing with you," Rae says to him again in a whisper.

Rae walks him down to almost the bottom of the library while talking to him. "So, what do you need to know about them? I have read all these books."

"Not really sure, that's why I was hoping to find info about them," James tells Rae.

"Is it for revenge?" Rae asks.

"Revenge for what?" James asks.

"For what they did to you the other day trying to find MEMPA," Rae tells James, getting excited.

"So, they are the ones that were here?" James says, confirming.

"Yeah, that's all anyone has been talking about," Rae tells him.

Rae stops almost at the same rack James found the prophecy book.

"Here is everything we have. Not much left after they left. They took most everything we had," Rae tells him.

"Thank you, you have been a very big help, Rae," James says with a smile.

"My pleasure. If you need anything else, anytime, you know where I'm at," Rae says to James with a smile.

"Will do, thanks again," James says to Rae.

James grabs the books and sits down. He starts looking at everything that he can find.

James reads how this group of people called SE is the most dangerous and deadly group anyone ever saw. The book shows the drawing of the mark they carry that is branded on their body. For centuries they have been trying to find MEMPA. MEMPA can change the outcome of the world. James reads as much as he can, then closes the books and takes them home.

As he walks past Rae, he says, "I'm going to borrow these. I'll bring them back as soon as I can."

Before Rae can say a word, James was already gone. James walks into the door of his home, slamming it behind him and putting the books on the table next to the door while looking at David.

David looks at him and asks, "What is going?"

"I need some info," James tells him.

"Okay, what do you want to know?" David asks.

"Explain a word to me," James says to David.

"Sure, what's the word," David asks.

James looks at David in the most serious way ever and says, "MEMPA."

David jumps up and starts walking around.

"David, what is it? I was told I got hurt because of it," James says, feeling scared.

"No, you didn't get hurt because of it. You got hurt because they we're looking for info on it," David tells James.

"What is it?" James asks.

"You are not ready for information. This is bigger than anything you could ever know," David tells James, almost with tears in his eyes.

"David, I got hurt for this without knowing what it is. I think I have earned the right to know," James says to David, putting his hand on his shoulder.

"You're right. MEMPA is the strongest power it the world. No one really knows what or where. Some say it can be found. Some say it's a being. SE was looking for any information for it because they want it for themselves. They feel with it they can take over the world. MEMPA is completely neutral magic, so anyone can use or control. Like I said though no one knows what it is," David explains to James.

"Would Miss Star know what it is?" James asks.

"No, I have already asked her. It's way before her time," David tells James.

They both sit down and try to figure out the next step.

CHAPTER 6

EXPECTATIONS

A few weeks have passed, and David has been meeting with the elders of the board. David refuses to discuss anything with James. All David will tell him is, when he needs to know they will tell him.

One morning David's mind is scattered, getting ready to go back to another meeting, when James asks, "What have you guys decided to do on finding out how SE came through our shield?"

David is moving around, trying to make sure he has everything he needs and looking around in the kitchen. "What do mean?" David asks.

James looks at David with a confused look and asks, "Aren't you guys trying to find out how they got through?"

David quickly says, "Yes, yes, we are." David looks at his watch and rushes out the door.

James walks into the kitchen with his dish and notices the David left his book. James sticks his head out the front door and shouts, "David, your book." He rushes to his room to grab his shoes and runs out the door, trying to give David his book. "David, David," James calls out, but David keeps going without stopping.

James is rushing through the streets, trying to get to David. He doesn't want to be too obvious, having people look at him. He had too much of that in the last few weeks with everything that has happened. Yet some people are still saying hi to James. He continues to power walk and wave. One man stops James to say thank you. As respectfully as possible James tells him he is welcome, however he is in a hurry. David walks into the Main Building. James keeps trying to get David's attention.

James follows David into the building, down the hallways, making turns that James did not know were even in the building. James is feeling like he is going through a big maze. Then James finally watches David go into a room when a girl, maybe fifteen to sixteen, walks up to James and says, "May I help you, James?"

James looks over at her and says, "Just here to give this book to David. I'm sorry to ask, but do I know you?"

The girl looks at him and smiles, saying, "James, it's me, Phoebe." James looks at her feeling lost but plays it off like he knew that.

"Oh yeah, I knew that. I was just messing you a little."

"You are such a kidder," Phoebe says to him. "What were you needing to do?"

"David forgot this book at home, and I'm bringing it to him," James tells Phoebe.

"Oh sure, that's fine. He went through there. Be careful," Phoebe tells James.

James starts walking to the room, turns his head, and says, "Thanks, Phoebe."

James walks up to the room and sees that it is no larger than a very small broom closet. He turns toward Phoebe, and she motions for him to go in. James takes a step forward when he suddenly feels like he is falling hundreds of feet, then stops at a very large door that looks hundreds of years old that is a little open. James looks through the door and sees everyone is in there. All the elders, Miss Star, and David are having the meeting David always attends. In this room it looks to have different-style flag with what looks to be family crest in the center of them. Each elder is wearing a robe with a symbol in the center. It looks like an infinity symbol with a *X* through it.

One of the elders asks David if he has told James anything.

"No, I haven't. I wouldn't know where to start," David responds.

"Good. That is not something that needs to come out right now," a second elder tells him.

"I don't understand why we can't tell him anything. He keeps asking, and it don't seem fair to keep this from him," David says with concern.

Then a third elder looks at David and says, "It doesn't matter what you think is fair. James doesn't need to know that his father was one of the men that broke through our shield. Can you imagine what that would do to us or what people would think?"

That moment James's heart stops. James starts thinking, *Now I understand why I wasn't allowed to know.*

Then James knocks and opens the door. The whole room falls into complete silence. James walks up to the table, throwing David his book, and says, "You left this on the counter at home, thought you might need it. Have a nice day."

David grabs his book, wanting to say thank you, but feeling like the time is not right. James starts walking out, when he asks, "James, how much did you hear?"

James stops in his tracks turns and says, "What does it matter? I know I don't mean anything." James walks out, closing the door behind him.

Phoebe looks at James with a smile and asks, "Was he happy?"

James just keeps walking as fast as he can, with his head down to avoid everyone.

David rushes out of the room to catch up to James. When he got through the door, James was already gone. David looks around in hope of catching James, but there was nobody around except for Phoebe.

"Did you see James come through here?" David asks.

"Yes, he rushed through looking very upset. Is everything okay?" Phoebe asks.

"Yes, everything is fine," David responds, walking back to the room where the meeting is.

"Well, how is James? What did he say?" Miss Star asks.

"I don't know. He was gone by the time I got to the door," David tells Miss Star.

Miss Star looks around at the table, upset at what happened.

"This is why I wanted to tell him way before anything like this happens. Things like this can't and never do stay hidden," David screams out right before walking out of the door.

"I agree with David. We should have told James after we found out," Miss Star says to the table.

"That is your choice. You are the boss, but we think it is a bad idea. Nobody that can destroy us like that should know anything about what they are or what they can do. He is half of them after all," an elder says.

"No, he is nothing like them. He is good. I have seen the goodness in him. They enjoy killing. He doesn't even like to hurt anyone," Miss Star says to the table.

The elders shut their mouths, looking around in shock. Miss Star sees the looks on their faces and walks out feeling outraged.

James is walking along the street back home in disbelief of what he just heard, trying to understand why his own godfather didn't tell him what was really going on. He asked so many times and nothing. As he is walking back, the same people are trying to say hello again but with no response from James. They can all see that he is very upset. James turns the corner, about to walk into his home, when he is grabbed from behind and disappears.

Five minutes later David comes around the corner and walks into his home looking for James.

"JAMES, you here? JAMES?" David screams out. David, feeling worried, steps out on the doorway, putting his face into his hands.

"What did I do? What did I..." David says to himself, while looking at the ground finding what appears to be James' necklace. David reaches out, in fear to check it. David picks up the necklace, and as he feared it is what he thought. David's heart starts racing in complete fear as he looks around.

David stands up and starts running straight to AJ's place. Running down the street with everyone looking at him, David arrives at AJ's home, knocking on the door, windows, even looking around the back, but with no sign of anyone around. David runs to the library, asking if anyone has seen James. David is going everywhere he knows James would be. David, scared of the worst possible things that could have happen to James, panics and runs to the lake where James, AJ, and Mari like to meditate. However, still nothing. David leans his back against the tree, face in his hands, and slides down, crying out in fear.

"Are you okay?" AJ asks David.

David looks and jumps up, seeing AJ, and says, "Oh, thank god. Have you seen James?"

"No, he was supposed to meet me a while ago, but he never showed up," AJ tells David.

"That's what I was scared of," David says, looking down in more fear.

"Why, David? What happened?" AJ asks.

David looks at AJ and tells him everything that happened and how James is nowhere to be found.

AJ looks at David and says, "I understand why James left. That is really messed up."

David looks at the lake, trying to think of something that could help. David quickly looks at AJ with tears in his eyes and asks, "You're his guardian. Can you check and see where he is at?"

AJ looks at David and says, "I don't if that a good idea. James might just be hiding. He might need some time." David then starts to beg AJ.

AJ gives David a look and tells him, "Okay, only because I'm starting to worry now and he is a best friend. Just promise me you won't say I told you."

David, feeling desperate, agrees.

AJ closes his eye and does a check to see where James is at. "That's not good," AJ says out loud.

"What's wrong?" David asks.

"Nothing," AJ tells him.

"You need to tell me what you see," David yells at AJ.

"No, that's what I'm telling you. I can't get a read on him," AJ tells David.

"What does that mean?" David asks, freaking out even more.

"That could mean two different things. Dead or somewhere unreachable," AJ tells David.

Tears run down David's cheek. "What are you not telling me?" AJ asks.

David holds up James's necklace. AJ's heart stops as he looks at the charm. AJ closes his eye again to try and see where he might be or what happened. After a few more seconds, AJ starts getting something.

"I see James outside your home. He looks very upset. He is turning the corner. What? Who is that?" AJ says.

"What? Who?" David asks.

"He got grabbed by someone. I don't know who that person is. Some guy grabbed him by his mouth and arms, then vanished. Everything cuts off from there," AJ says.

David looks at AJ and says, "We need to tell Miss Star."

They both rush to her office. They get to her doorway, which is now back to the slot it was, and knock.

"Miss Star, it's David. We need to talk right away," David shouts. Next thing they know they are all in her office. Inside the office they see Miss Star and all the elders.

David walks up to Miss Star's desk and says, "James has been taken."

Miss Star looks at David and asks, "What do you mean, taken?"

"I saw someone take him. David asked me if I saw James, and I did a search for him and saw someone take him," AJ tells her.

"Who would take James?" Miss Star asks.

AJ, looking around the room, sees one person who looks familiar. AJ walks over to him slowly while Miss Star is talking about ways to find out where James might be. Miss Star looks at AJ with a look on her face. AJ walks down to someone looking at his hand. He has the same marks he saw on the man that took James.

AJ looks back at Miss Star and asks, "What do you think about"?

AJ grabs the elder, yelling, "Who are you?"

"AJ, that is Jeffrey, an elder," Miss Star shouts.

"Then why did I see him grab James," AJ responds.

"That's impossible. Are you sure?" Miss Star asks.

"Yes, I'm sure," AJ tells her.

"I don't know what you think you saw, kid, but you saw wrong," Jeffrey says to AJ.

During this commotion, Phoebe comes into the room from behind a curtain and puts her hand on Jeffrey's head. In seconds Phoebe looks at him and says, "You should be ashamed of yourself."

She looks at everyone. "He has been working with SE looking for MEMPA. He is why they came here. Helped them get past our shield. He grabbed James and took him to a place I'm not sure what it was. He wants to use MEMPA."

James opens his eyes and finds himself in a dark place. He looks around while staying where he is at. With light coming only from a window above him, he cannot tell where he is at. Looks like it might have been an older house, maybe built in the eighteenth century. The house looks large with some brick, mostly wood. The room he is in is completely empty. James stands up slowly when he notices that the window is up high in this room. James jumps to try and get a look at where he might be. All he can see is he is in a basement. James closes his eye in hope to be able to reach or send out a signal to AJ for help. The door slowly opens with a creaking sound. James jumps back in a fight position.

A man with a limp, no hair, and brown eyes walks into the room with a plate of food in his hand. The man turns his head, looking around the room, and snaps his fingers. A table and chair pop up out of nowhere. The man looks up, snaps again, then a light pops up so they could see better. The man motions for James to sit and eat.

James looks at the man and says, "What is that poison, or maybe a potion to get me to talk? I won't touch it. I'll never say anything."

The man hangs his head down in a way to say, "That hurt my feelings."

James looks at him and notices that this man is not evil. If he is, he doesn't know it.

The man picks up the plate and starts walking out with his head still down.

James looks at him feeling bad and says, "Hey, I'm sorry. I'm on edge right now. Did you make this?" James points at the food. The man nods his head yes.

"Okay, I'll eat it. Thank you," James says, feeling bad.

The man lifts his head up with a smile, placing the plate back down on the table.

"Do you speak?" James asks.

The man shakes his head no.

"I'm James. What is your name?" James asks.

The man bends down to the ground and in the dirt spells "B O B."

"Your name is Bob. Can I call you Bobby?" James asks. Bob nods his head yes very quickly and happily.

James sits down at the table, and as Bob is walking out, James turns to him and says, "Thank you. Oh, can I get some water, please." Bob smiles and snaps. James finds a glass of water sitting next to the plate on the table.

A little while later James is still sitting at the table, all food and water gone. James is trying to understand what happened. After finding out everything about his father, was he being punished for walking in? Is this what happens when you know too much?

Bob comes back in to collect the plate and glass. James sits up to look at Bob and thanks him again for the food. Bob nods his head and smiles and starts to walk away when James reaches out to grab Bob's arm. James looks at Bob and asks, "Is there any way you can tell me where we are or why I'm here?"

Bob shakes his head to say no.

"I thought we were friends. You made me this great meal, and all I want to know is where I might be, please," James continues to ask.

Bob sticks his head out of the door, looking around, and, with a large amount of concern, smiles at James, bends down, and writes "C A L." Then Bob jumps up.

"What's wrong? Why did you…" James asks when another man walks into the room.

"Hello, Bob, how are you today?" the second man says, smiling. Bob smiles and nods his head.

"Can I get a minute with James, please?" the man asks Bob.

Bob nods his head, smiles, then waves to James as he leaves the room. The man closes the door behind Bob.

James steps into a fighting position, ready for anything that might happen.

The man, dark hair and eyes, looks at James and says, "Really, James, I'm not going to hurt you. My name is Benjamin. Please call me Ben."

Benjamin puts his hand out as a sign of respect.

James looks at him, unsure what to do, and slowly moves his hand out.

Benjamin reaches out and shakes James hand. "It is very nice to meet you," Benjamin says to James.

James, feeling confused, says, "Thank you. I'm not sure what to think. Can you tell me where I'm at?"

"Well, I can tell you that you are somewhere in Northern California. I can also tell you that you are unable to call any of your help or guardian because we have a magic shield on this place just so nobody can see through whether magic or otherwise," Benjamin tells James.

"Why am I here?" James asks.

"Well, you are here because someone wanted you gone," Benjamin tells James.

"Who?" James asks.

"Elder. As a matter of fact, he is the one who put you here," Benjamin says.

James looks down in disbelief.

Benjamin looks at James and says, "Sorry, kid, it happens."

Benjamin turns to walk out when he looks at James and says, "I was once in your shoes. They threw me out because of my family. Not fair, but bloodline plays a lot in the world."

James quickly stops Benjamin from leaving and says, "I don't know anything about my family. I was raised by my godfather. Why would anything like bloodline matter in this situation?"

"James, it matters because..." Benjamin starts to say when another man walks up. "Boss, we have a problem. He's back," the man says.

"I'll be right there," Benjamin tells him.

Benjamin starts leaving the room when James shouts, "WAIT! Please finish what you were saying."

Benjamin turns back into the room and says, "James, it matters because I'm your father."

CHAPTER

NEW LOOK

A day has passed, and James is still in the same room. He has been sitting in the chair that Bob gave him, trying to understand the fact he just learned who his father is, wondering why he wasn't around. He starts to think about everything that he was told by Miss Star, the prophecy he heard about. Could this be him? Is that why it called to him? Is that why it called to him? Is that why he was the one to found the book? What is really going on?

Bob walks into the room with more food and a smile.

"Bobby, is there anything we can do about me in this room?" James asks.

Bob puts a finger up to say hold on. Bob walks out of the room for a few minutes and returns with Benjamin following.

Benjamin walks up to James and responds to James, "I was told you have a question."

"Why am I in this room? You can't keep me here, you know. If I'm really your son, why would you lock me away like this?" James asks.

"Who said anything about locked away. Th ere is no lock on the door, look," Benjamin tells James.

James walks over to the door, and the only door handle on the door is one to keep it closed. "You mean to tell me this time I could have left this room," James says.

"Yes, you are my son. I have no reason to lock you away. I have been waiting for you to come out," Benjamin says with a smile.

James steps outside of the room. He turns, looking at Benjamin, and asks, "What if I try to run?"

Benjamin places his hand of the back of James's neck and tells him, "That is up to you. If you want to leave, good luck. If you stay with me, I'll be happy to have you here."

James thinks, *that this is too easy.*

"Yes, it is too easy, but that's the way it is. Plus, I would love to give those elders something to stress about," Benjamin says.

"How did you know what I was thinking?" James asks.

"That's my gift. I hear everyone's thoughts," Benjamin tells James.

Benjamin starts walking James outside to show him the land. As they are walking through the house, James is seeing nothing that says hatred or any kind of evil. James is looking around at all the people and notices that they all have the SE mark on the back of their necks.

"Ben, what is that symbol on everyone's neck?" James asks.

Benjamin looks at him with shame on his face and says, "That is the symbol for our people here. SE also known as the—"

"Spawns of Evil," James says.

"Yes, that's right," Benjamin says.

"You don't have one, why is that?" James asks.

"In order to get that mark on your body, you have to kill an innocent," Benjamin tells James.

James, with a look of confusion, asks, "Wait, you have never killed an innocent?"

Benjamin says no to James with a smile.

They both walk out the front door of a house that looks to be a castle in the center of the grounds. They walk the land, and James is looking at this place in amazement.

James looks at Benjamin and asks, "How did you know who I was?"

"Well, the moment I saw you in the Main Building after one of my men hit you with a knockout spell, which I did not tell him to do for the record. You look just like your mother. That's how I knew. Plus, the way you came out trying to stop intruders, who you have no idea what they could do to you—that is all me," Benjamin says with a smile.

They walk to the outskirts of the land and sit on the root of a large tree. James, with his heart racing, looks at Benjamin and asks, "I always wanted to know, but no one was there able to answer this question, who is my mother?"

Benjamin looks at James with shock and tells him, "James, you don't know who your mother is? James, your mother is—"

AJ pops in, grabs James, and disappears.

Benjamin jumps to his feet and screams out, "NO! I WILL GET HIM BACK."

AJ and James are back on the island. James is trying to comprehend what just happened.

"WHAT DID YOU DO?" James screams at AJ, grabbing his shirt.

AJ, unsure, asks, "What do you mean? I just saved your life."

"No, I was fine. Take me back," James tells AJ.

"What do you mean? I can't do that. Who was that?" AJ asks.

"That was my—" James starts to say when David walks up to James, wrapping his arms around him tightly, saying, "I'm so sorry. I should have told you."

"Don't worry about it. I was with him," James tells David.

"Wait, what? With who?" AJ asks.

James looks at AJ and tells him, "I was with my father."

David's heart stops for second, and he asks, "Why were you with him?"

"An elder took me there because I guess he didn't want me here," James tells them.

David puts his hand on James's shoulder, looks into his eyes, and says, "That elder has been dealt with. He thought because of who you are and who your father is that you were just like him. Even Miss Star said that you are good. We all know it too."

Mari runs up to James, hugging him on contact. "Oh my gosh, I'm so glad you're okay. I've been so worried about you. What happened?" Mari says in tears.

"I was taken to my father," James tells Mari.

"Really, who is he? Wait, isn't he…" Mari looks around, then continues, "You are home and safe now." Mari looks at AJ and David.

"We need to let Miss Star know he is back."

Almost out of nowhere Miss Star pops up behind them. "I see you have safely made it back. Welcome home, James," Miss Star says.

James looks at her, knowing it was an elder that did this to him, wondering if it was under her orders.

"James, may I have a word with you, please?" Miss Star asks. Feeling like he has no choice, James agrees.

James and Miss Star walk away from everyone toward the lake.

"I'm sure you have questions like, why did this happen? Even, who told him to do it? I can ensure you that I had nothing to do with your disappearance. That's why you bought back the way you were. The moment AJ felt you, he jumped to get you. I'm very happy you're safe," Miss Star explains. Then she gives James a very big hug, then pulls off to try and be professional.

"Did you know where I was?" James asks.

"Yes, only after because Phoebe told me. She read the mind of the elder," Miss Star tells him.

James gives a confused look.

Miss Star explains, "Phoebe can read minds with a single touch."

"So, you know I was with my father," James says.

"Yes, I know," Miss Star says.

"Then maybe you can answer a question for me, seeing how I was taken as I was about to be told. Can you tell me anything about my mother?" James asks with a stern voice.

Miss Star looks at him with concern immediately written all over her face.

James starts to walk away.

Miss Star looks at him with tears and says, "Wait."

"I'm sorry, but I have gone my whole life without really knowing or thinking about my parents. I did everything I could to survive. Then my father, a person I didn't know was alive, comes out from nowhere and right as I'm about to find out who my mother is, I'm bought back here. Can you tell me, or do you choose not to? To be honest it feels like you know something and don't want me to know anything," James says with tears pouring down his face.

"My dear boy, it's not that I don't want you to know. The truth is…" Miss Star tells James as tears start running down her face.

AJ and Mari run to Miss Star in a panic, saying, "We have a problem." Miss Star and James follow AJ and Mari with Miss Star telling James, "We will continue this later, I promise."

They get to a mysterious bag left out of nowhere in front of the Main Building. Unsure what it could be inside, Miss Star tells everyone to stay back. She slowly bends down to open the bag and hears a cry of pain from inside. Miss Star quickly opens the bag to find former elder Jeffrey inside inches from death.

Miss Star screams out, "Someone get the doctor."

AJ runs to get the doctor as fast as he can. Miss Star takes Jeffrey's hand and tries to keep him with her.

"I'm sorry. I didn't mean for all this," Jeffrey says to Miss Star. "Don't worry, Jeffrey. We are getting you help," Miss Star says to him.

"Estrella, it's too late. I'm sorrrrryyy," Jeffrey says with his last breath.

Miss Star drops her head, knowing Jeffrey has passed away. She looks up and says, "We need to find out who did this and how they got in here."

Everyone starts moving to get it done. The doctor shows up, and Miss Star tells her, "I want a funeral for Jeffrey, despite what he did. He died in my arms, and I have known him my whole life. Tomorrow we honor him."

The doctor takes his body to prepare him. Miss Star stands up and looks at her people. She lifts herself in the air about five feet and says, "This is not okay. You might know what happened and that James was taken from us a day ago. He is now back, but in return we get our elder in a bag. If anyone of you thinks for a second that this is his fault for any reason, take that out of your head right now! Our friend is gone. That is the fault of the person who put him there. We will do whatever it takes to keep you all safe. We will not let Jeffrey die in vain. If you can help, please do so." Miss Star lowers herself back down to the ground.

The next day around dusk, everyone comes together near the lake in remembrance of the fallen elder Jeffrey. James stands on the outside on a rooftop, watching, unsure if this is right after what he did to everyone. Jeffrey is wrapped up and placed on a table. At the moment Miss Star and the elders are forming a circle around Jeffrey.

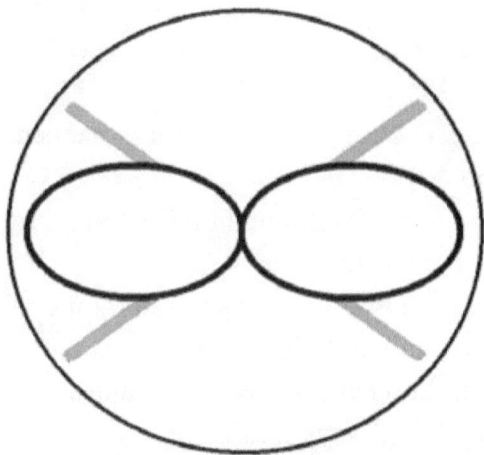

Together they magically raise him up. At the same time, they all say, "Rest in peace," with their hands out. With all their magic together, the symbol on the robes and their hands turn bright with light. After a few seconds the body of Jeffrey is now gone with nothing left behind. James turns with some tears in his eyes and walks away.

James is walking back home when he hears something from inside of the trees. Thinking everyone was at the funeral, he says, "Hello." James doesn't see anything. He turns to head back home when he is grabbed again. James is pulled into the trees, where he realizes he was just grabbed by Benjamin.

James, in disbelief, asks, "How are you here?" James gives him hug.

"You didn't think I would stay away, did you?" Benjamin says, still hugging James.

"I'm happy to see you, but I don't hear any alarm. How did you get here?" James asks.

"The alarm is only for evil, if you have killed. I have never killed. Plus, I'm still considered part of this family too. I was thrown out, but it never really took effect because I never joined the family business in full," Benjamin says to James.

Seeing everything as said, James can see the truth in front of him.

Benjamin can see everything what is happening by the lake and asks, "Who died?"

"Jeffrey, an elder. We found him in a bag in front of the Main Building," James tells him.

"I wanted to know if you wanted to come with me. That is one reason why I'm here," Benjamin tells James.

"I can't, but I do have a question," James tells Benjamin.

"Okay, anything," says Benjamin.

James takes a deep breath and asks, "Before I was grabbed, you were about to tell me who my mother is. Can you tell me now?"

Benjamin looks at James and says, "Well, only if you think you can handle it. Your mother, I met her here. She was part of the family who runs this place."

"Are you telling me that Miss Star is my mother?" James asks. "Estrella, no. She is your mother's older sister. She loved me though. When we got married, she helped us. When you were born, Estrella was so proud to have you around. Your mother's name is Marcelin. She is the love of my life," Benjamin explains to

James. "Benjamin, can you tell me what happened to her?" James asks.

> *"We were happy together. Everything was great. Until one night when I was asked to do something I didn't want to do. I was told to kill an innocent. I wouldn't do it. They tried to make me do it, but I got away from it. I returned home to find your mother had vanished. When I found out that she went back to her family, I went to get her back. Estrella told me where she was. I almost had her back when my family found out where I was at and what I was doing. To stop me from what they felt would be a mistake, they started killing people. Then a war broke out. We got you to safety with your mother's guardian, who was also her best friend. You know him as your godfather David. When the boat blew up, we thought we had lost you. She tried to go in after you, but then the person who destroyed the boat hit her with a death spell (aqha death tonl). She died in my arms. I was forced to go with my family. However, to make sure your mother is still with me, I never kill,"* Benjamin tells James.

James wipes the tears from his eyes.

Benjamin hears someone walking their way. Benjamin looks at James and says, "I'm sorry, someone's coming. I need to go."

"Wait, will I see you again?" James asks.

"I promise," Benjamin says with his hand on James's face. Then Benjamin disappears into the dark.

AJ walks up and asks, "Everything okay, bro?"

James wipes the tears off his face and says, "Yeah, I'm good."

AJ looks at James and says, "Okay, we have been looking for you."

Mari walks up to James and asks, "Why were you in there?"

"Just staying clear away from everyone. Took some time away to clear my head," James tells her.

Mari looks at AJ, and he smiles. "Okay, if you say so," Mari says to them.

"Are we still on for tonight?" AJ asks.

"Of course, we are," James says.

"Good, I do not want you be yourself after everything that has happened to you," Mari says to James.

They start to walk over to James's home.

Later that night they are all asleep. Everything is quiet. James is dreaming about everything his father said. To know where he comes from is a blessing. Then James is seeing the house he was in, where his father is at. He can see Jeffrey, the former elder, standing in a room with his father walking into the room.

"They know what I did," Jeffrey tells Benjamin.

Benjamin tells him, "You got what you wanted. I did to. What do you want me to do?"

"I need your help to make this go away. I need you to get rid of Phoebe and Estrella," Jeffrey says.

"No, I told you they will not get hurt. This is your problem not mine. I did my part. Now you need to deal with the karma you made," Benjamin says as he turns to walk out of the room.

"You do not walk away from me."

Benjamin turns back with dark a look on his face, then laughs and says, "Did you forget who I am. I'm not that little kid you would talk down to. This is my house."

Benjamin looks at his men. "Please show Jeffrey the door. I have my son here. Because of you I would never have known he was alive."

The men walk Jeffrey out of the room. Benjamin turns around and shouts, "JAMES!"

James wakes up suddenly, looking around at Mari and AJ. Mari looks at James, asking, "Are you okay?"

James nods his head, wiping the sweat off his head.

"What happened? I know you saw something," Mari asks.

"I saw what happened to Jeffrey," James tells Mari.

"Was it who I think it was?" Mari asks.

"Not in the way you think. He was nice about it. I saw everything. He asked his men to see Jeffrey to the door. It was his men that did it. He had nothing to do with it," James explains.

AJ stands up, saying, "We need to make sure that Miss Star knows." Mari and James look at each other and say, "Agreed."

The next morning the three of them went to see Miss Star. On their way to the Main Building, James notices an old man who everyday says hello to him. James walks up to him to give his condolences for Jeffrey.

"I'm very sorry for the loss of Jeffrey," James says to the old man.

The old man smiles and tells James, "I'm just glad you're okay."

"Thank you." James smiles.

AJ and Mari walk up to them. AJ tells James, "We got to get to her office. What are you doing?"

"I'm taking to him. Anyways, sir, I'm sorry again. Have a nice day," James says with a smile, walking away. James looks at AJ with annoyance and asks, "What the hell, bro? That was disrespectful." AJ looks at James confused and says, "What are you talking about?"

"The older man I was just talking to, you disrespected him," James tells AJ, getting mad.

AJ looks back to where James was just at, and no one is there.

"James, there is nobody there," AJ tells him.

James looks back and can still see the old man. "No, he is right there," James tells AJ.

AJ, realizing what is happening, looks back and says, "You're right, James. Sir, I'm very sorry for my lack of respect."

James thinks for a minute and asks, "AJ, was there anyone really there."

AJ takes a deep breath and responds, "No. However, last year we had a very sweet older man who lived there. He always said hi to everyone. We all loved him. His name was Eugene, or as he was known by everyone around here, Uncle Gene. He had no family, so we all gave him one," AJ explains.

James looks back and waves again. "Wait a minute, are you telling me that I can see…" James starts to say when they run into Miss Star.

"Miss Star, may we please speak to you," Mari asks.

"Unless this is something important," Miss Star says.

"Oh, it is. It's about Jeffrey," Mari tells her.

Miss Star looks up at them and tells them, "My office."

They walk into the Main Building and down the hallway. As they are getting closer to the slot, they find themselves in her office like nothing happened. They all have a seat at her desk, and Mari says, "Okay, James, tells her about your dream."

James is looking at Miss Star, and the only thing he can think is how she like his aunt, his mother's older sister. He wants to ask so many questions about his mother. What was she like as a kid? What did she look like?

"James, James," Mari says repeatedly.

Miss Star looks at James and asks, "James, are you okay?"

AJ, knowing what is in his head, says as he smacks the table, getting James out of the trance he is in, "James just found out about another gift he has."

Miss Star, with shock on her face, says, "Oh, okay. We can talk about that in a minute."

James wipes his eye and says, "I'm sorry, where were we?"

"We would like you to tell me about your dream?" Miss Star says.

James explains his dream. Miss Star, knowing that James can see things, looks amazed that he can see things in this way.

After their meeting Miss Star thanked them all for the information. Knowing who and why everything happened to Jeffrey can now help her do her job. As everyone is leaving, Miss Star asks James to stay for a minute.

Mari looks at James and asks, "Do you want me to wait?"

James looks at her and says, "No, thank you. I'll catch up with you later."

Mari nods her head as she and AJ leave the office.

Miss Star looks at James and asks, "So tell me what's going on?"

James looks at her nervously and asks, "What do you mean?"

Miss Star looks at him and asks, "What is the new gift?"

"Oh, yeah that. The older man down the road, the one who I guess passed away last year, I saw him and had a conversation," James says with a smile.

Miss Star has a look on her face, and with tears in her eyes, she stands up from her chair and asks, "Are you telling me that you can see the spirits?"

"Yes, that is what I'm saying. I didn't know about it until today. Why is that such a big deal?" James asks.

Miss Star can barely look at him when she says, "I once knew someone that could do that too."

James looks at her and asks, "May I ask who?"

Still with her back turned, she says to James, "My younger sister." James wants to cry but is holding it back.

Miss Star continues to say, "She was my best friend. I watched over her the best I could, you know. All I ever wanted was for her to be happy. She had more gift than anyone I ever seen. She was the strongest witch I ever saw. She married the man of her dreams, and the day we lost her, I lost everything. No matter who I had around, it was never the same. I miss her every single day."

Miss Star wipes the tears from her own face, turning around, facing James. "I'm sorry, that is way too much about me. Off you go," Miss Star says to James, pulling him out of the office.

She sits at her desk, opens up a drawer of her desk, and pulls out a picture of her with Marcelina. "I wish you were her with me. I'm so lost without you," Miss Star says, crying, holding the picture to her chest.

CHAPTER

THE OTHER SIDE

A few weeks have passed since Jeffrey was killed. The murderer is still unknown. James has been waiting for any word from his father with no luck. Life kept moving for everyone. James and David have reconnected despite everything that happened.

With everything that is happening to James, Mari starts to wonder about her parents. All Mari has ever known is her aunt, and she never thought to ask.

Mari gets up after a long night of no sleep. Her aunt Fran

greets her like normal as she walks into the kitchen for breakfast. Mari sits at the table looking lost. Fran places a plate of food on the table in front of her, but Mari doesn't even attempt to reach out.

"Are you feeling okay?" Fran asks.

"Yes, I feel fi ne. I have been thinking about something, and I am scared to ask about it," Mari tells Fran.

Fran, with a loving smile on her face, looks at Mari and tells her, "You can ask me anything."

"Anything?" Mari asks.

"Anything. Nothing is off limits," Fran tells her.

Fran turns back to the stove to get herself some food.

Mari's heart is racing when she asks, "What can you tell me about my parents?"

Fran drops her plate on the floor, breaking the plate.

Mari jumps up to help. "Are you okay?"

"I'm sorry, sweetheart. The plate got away from me," Fran says to Mari.

Fran sits Mari down at the table to explain. She sits across from Mari with tears in her eyes. Fran takes Mari's hand and starts to explain.

> "Your parents were the most incredible, bighearted people I had met. When you were born, they loved you so much. They didn't have much money, but if they had it or could get it, you had it. This is where we are all from. Your mother and your father, my big brother, knew each other for a long time. They were always together. Your father, even when we were kids, loved having me around. Their names were Ashley and John. I remember when they were pregnant with you, they couldn't decide on a name. You mother was in labor with you, and there were complications. You weren't breathing. With your parent

scared for your life, a nurse started to do CPR. After fifteen minutes, everyone told her to stop. You were brain dead. She wouldn't stop until you started crying. When you started crying, she handed you to your mother, who saw the nurse's name tag. That's where your name came from."

"Aunt Fran, what does have to do with everything?" Mari asks.

"You wanted to know, so that's what I'm telling you," Fran responds.

"Okay, you right. What happened to them?" Mari asks.

"We had a war break out here, and they were trying to help people when they got caught in the crossfire," Fran tells her.

"Is that it?" Mari asks.

"That's all I can say for now," Fran tells Mari.

Mari, feeling incomplete, doesn't understand. "Why is that all you can tell me?" Mari asks.

Fran gets up and says, "I'm sorry. I love you, but I can't tell you anymore." Fran rushes out of the room.

Mari is left sitting at the table wondering why she had to stop.

Meanwhile, Benjamin is sitting in his room at a desk, looking at a photo, thinking about what happened when he last saw his son James, the way James was still in the dark about everything. Benjamin could understand not knowing about this world and everything in it but to not know about his family. David should have told him something. The fact that James last name isn't even the same anymore. When did his name turn from Spawns to Frye? James should have his father's last name. Then Benjamin realizes he is looking for a reason to be mad for something he asked for a long time ago.

The door opens with one of the Benjamin's men walking in and says, "Boss, your father is here."

"Okay, thank you. By the way, I was told something. Do you know what happened to that elder Jeffrey," Benjamin asks?

The man looks away from Benjamin, thinking, *oh yeah*, and says, "No, sir."

Benjamin walks up to him and asks, "Are you sure?" "Yes, sir," the man says.

Benjamin looks at him again and tells him, "You know the one thing I hate more than anything." "What's that, sir?" the man says.

Benjamin grabs him by his neck and lifts him as far as his arm can each and shouts, "BEING LIED TO."

Then the man starts screaming while he catches on fire. Benjamin throws him, not to get burned. Benjamin turns away from his father, who set the man on fire, killing him.

Benjamin's father, Joseph, a very old man with no hair and very dark eyes, looks at him and says with his eye black as night, "You never could do what you needed to. I saw the elder and took care of it.

I made sure that they got the message."

Benjamin gives a look of desperation, telling Joseph, "What message? You didn't need to do that. Trust goes further than fear."

"There you go again being naïve," Joseph tells Benjamin.

Benjamin tries to walking away, then freezes in place. He is lifted into the air and flips him upside down, turning him back around.

Joseph walks up to him, putting his finger on Benjamin's head, and tells him, "I tell you when you can leave. You may have control and the house, but I still run everything."

Joseph walks away from Benjamin, leaving him in the same place. When Joseph closes the door, Benjamin falls out of the air, landing on his head and shoulders.

Joseph is walking down the hall when another one of the men

accidentally bump into him. "Sir, I am so sorry," the man says, bowing at his feet.

Joseph looks at this man and asks him, "Do you know how many people I have killed?"

With his head still down, the man says, "No, sir, but I know it has been a lot."

Joseph laughs at that comment and tells the man, "This is true."

Joseph's eyes then turn black with what looks to be a part of his soul stepping out of his body and steps into the man's body.

With the man possessed with part of Joseph's soul, he says, "This way it looks like a suicide, and I don't need to clean up myself."

The man then shouts, "Aqha death tonl," with a green light coming from his own hand, killing himself.

Benjamin, watching his father kill another person, decides he needs to do something. Benjamin walks through the house to the outside. Trying not to be seen, he rushes to the outskirt of the land to the same tree that he and James sat. Feeling sick to his stomach, he tries to catch a breath. Benjamin wants to try and see James again but unsure on how to get through to him. Benjamin tries to send a message to a witch he knows well.

Benjamin closes his eyes, saying in his head, "Hey, can you hear me?"

"Of course, I can," says another voice.

"I need your help," Benjamin asks.

"What do you need?" another voice says.

"I need to talk to James," Benjamin says.

"No, I will not let you do that," another voice says.

"Please, things are about to get very bad. I fear my father knows he might be alive, or worse, where he is," Benjamin explains. "What do you expect me to do, take you to his home for a sit down?" another voice tells him.

"No, just have him meet me in the forest after everyone is sleeping," Benjamin explains.

"What? I can't do that. Wait, how did you...? You've already done that, didn't you?" another voice asks.

"Yes, but you never knew. That should say I'm still not evil," Benjamin says.

"When did you do that?" another voice asks.

"Jeffrey's funeral," Benjamin says.

"Let me see what I can do. I don't know how much I like this," another voice says.

"I know, but he is my boy," Benjamin says.

"Not that. The fact that my guardian can get into my head after all this time," another voice says.

"You love that. I think the part you don't like is the fact that your guardian is also your brother-in-law. Thank you, Estrella," Benjamin says.

Miss Star stands there with a concerned look on her face.

The next morning Mari walks into the kitchen and says good morning to Fran. Fran stands up, walking past Mari without a word. Mari looks at Fran acting this way and walks straight into the room Fran went into. Fran lies down, trying to avoid Mari.

Mari sits at the foot of the bed and starts bouncing, telling Fran, "I will not leave or stop until you talk to me. You always said we work out all problems. That is what keeps a family strong."

Fran looks at Mari and says, "I cannot talk about it."

"If that is the issue, I will not ask again. Nothing is worth not having you," Mari tells Fran.

Fran smiles, sitting up and hugging Mari. "Now let's go eat breakfast," Mari says to Fran. They both stand up and walk into the kitchen.

Benjamin sends a message to Miss Star asking her if she has set up a meeting. Benjamin sits on the large tree waiting for her to answer until he hears her say, "Tonight at midnight. Same place."

Benjamin, feeling excited, walks into the house, preparing for the night. He opens a desk drawer, pulling out a picture of James's mother and him. Benjamin places it into a bag with a few other things of hers so James could get to know his mother Marcelina. Later that night Benjamin starts to walk out of his room when Bobs walk up to him, asking him if he is leaving.

Benjamin takes his hands and says, "No, little brother, I'm going to see James. I will be back."

Bob smiles and hugs Benjamin tightly.

"I need to go. I'll see you later, okay?" Benjamin tells Bob in a whisper.

Bob waves good-bye to Benjamin as he walks away.

Benjamin pops up on the island, in the place he was told to be at. Benjamin is looking around the trees for James when Miss Star pops out from the shadows.

"Estrella, what are you doing here? Where is James?" Benjamin asks.

"He is not coming. I don't know what you are trying to do, but I can't let him get hurt," Miss Star says.

"Hurt? Who is getting hurt here other than me? Last I checked, the only reason I even know he is alive is because your elder brought him to me," Benjamin says to Miss Star.

"You know I had nothing to do with that. I was trying to keep him safe and hidden. Last I checked, I didn't kill the elder," Miss Star says to Benjamin.

"I didn't kill, or have anything to do with that. My father did because he felt I was being too soft," Benjamin says, feeling upset about it.

Miss Star looks at Benjamin and says, "I know you had nothing to do with it. I'm sorry, but I don't want anything happen to James. Too much for too long," Miss Star explains.

Benjamin looks at Miss Star, lifting a bag, asking, "Then can you give this to James for me?"

Miss Star takes the bag, opening it, and asks, "What is this?"

All she can see are pictures of Marcelina and things that were hers as well.

Miss Star starts to tear up, asking, "Where did you get all this?"

"When she left, this is everything she left behind," Benjamin says.

Miss Star stares at Benjamin for a minute and says, "You really do care for him."

"Yes, I do," Benjamin says to her.

Miss Star looks at Benjamin and tells him, "No, I will not give this to James. You can do it tomorrow. I will set something up." Benjamin grabs Miss Star in a large hug, thanking her.

"Don't make me regret this," Miss Star tells him.

"You won't, I promise," Benjamin says, feeling extremely happy.

The next morning Miss Star sends for James to come to her office. While she is waiting, she is feeling extremely nerves about what could happen. How will James react to the news? Miss Star is moving things around in her office. Knock, knock at the door and Miss Star's heart is now racing even more. Before anyone could speak, James finds himself in her office.

"I was told you wanted to see me," James says, feeling very nervous as well.

Miss Star, who is now sitting at her desk with a straight face, says to James, "Yes, we need to talk."

James looks at Miss Star, wondering what she might say.

"James, something has come to my attention, and we need to talk about it," Miss Star tells James.

James starts, trying to say, "If this is about—"

Miss Star jumps in, cutting James off. "James, please let me tell you." James sits back with his mouth closed.

"Okay, that day you heard, I mean…" Miss Star is having

a hard time trying to explain to him. "I want you to know that I am…" Miss Star can't get the words out.

"Miss Star, are you—" James tries helping but still gets cut off by Miss Star.

"Please, James, I need to say this," Miss Star tells James, starting to tear up.

James can see the tears and jumps to help. "Aunt Estrella…"

She turns to him. "Yes, James, wait, you called me…" Miss Star says in tears.

"Yes, I did. I know. I understand that what you are trying to say and how you couldn't find the words," James tells her.

Miss Star grabs him in a very large hug with tears running down her face, asking, "How long have you known? Who told you? Why didn't you say anything?"

James looks at her and says, "I was told the night of Jeffrey's funeral by Benjamin, who happens to be my father and your brother-in-law. Now I have question for you now that it's all out."

Miss Star, feeling as though all the weight has been lifted off her shoulder, smiles and asks, "What would my nephew like to know?"

James looks at her and finally asks, "What can you tell me about my mother? What did she look like?"

Miss Star jumps to pull out a picture of her and his mother. James looks at the picture, tearing up, and smiles, saying, "I can't believe after all this time I can now see my mother. She is the most beautiful woman I had ever seen." James feels like he saw her somewhere before though. Not that long ago.

Miss Star puts her arm around James and says, "We were the best of friends, growing up. She was so incredible. When I first saw you, I thought you might be. However, I wasn't sure until I was told your father was here. That was when I knew it was you. My sister's son. I'm sorry that I didn't say anything earlier. I just didn't know how to." Miss Star looks into his eyes.

"I understand why you waited," James tells her.

"James, tonight I would like to set something up," Miss Star tells him.

"Okay, what?" James asks.

"I would like to—" Miss Star starts saying when the alarm sounds.

They both rush outside to find out what is happening. People are running down the street in fear.

"What is going on?" Miss Star asks.

One of the people points and keeps running.

"James, we need to finish this shortly."

James nods, and Miss Star starts running down the street to find out what it is scaring everyone. James, feeling like he must help, starts running to catch up.

"What are you doing? Get out of here," Miss Star yells at James.

"No, this is my home and you're my family. Nobody hurts my family," James responds.

Miss Star smiles, and they keep running toward the danger. Then they see what is causing all the panic—a forty-foot-long snake-type creature with three different head (a tiger, an alligator, and a snake).

This creature is destroying homes just by sliding along. James and Miss Star stand side by side looking at this creature when James shouts, asking, "What is that thing?"

"That's a triple-fang snake," Miss Star tells him.

James takes off his necklace, putting into his pocket, and tells her, "Step back a little. It's about to get very hot."

Miss Star steps back a little as James closes his eyes. The triple fang snake looks at James and can sense the heat coming from him. The snake head in the middle moves to strike at James when his body turns into a stream of fire, completely destroying the head and the neck. Miss Star, looking at James, can't believe what she is seeing. After the middle head was destroyed, the other two moves to attack at the same time.

James, who is still on fire, makes sure the other two heads meet the same fate as the first. The body is burned to ashes within seconds as well.

Miss Star walks up to James as his fire is calming down and can see his eyes are still black. However, they are returning to normal. Miss Star asks him, "Are you okay? I didn't know you were that strong."

James looks at her and responds, "I'm fine. Are you okay? I was worried about you."

"I'm fine and you just...wow," Miss Star says, smiling.

"Well, I didn't want anyone getting hurt," James tells her, a little out of breath.

Miss Star gets a looks on her face that looks as though she was just talking to her sister. "What?" James asks.

"You sound just like your mother," Miss Star tells him.

James smiles, and they walk back toward the Main Building when James hears, "KOUNT," sending Miss Star flying.

James turns around to stop whoever is using the spell just to find himself being hit with the same spell.

Coming around the corner of the Main Building, straight down the street, watching everything happen, Rae shouts, "Hey, who are you?"

The man looks her way, and a green light flies her way. Rae goes out of the way, and the side of the building is knocked out. Rae looks up and watches another man, much older, grab James's hand while he is on the ground, knocked out, then vanishing. However, Miss Star is left behind on the ground, knocked out as well.

Rae runs to Miss Star, checking on her. "Miss Star, Miss Star, are you okay?" Rae asks, kneeling on the ground next to Miss Star. Rae starts shaking her to try wake her up.

AJ is running toward them after feeling something had happened.

Miss Star wakes up in fear for James. "Where is James?" Miss Star asks.

Rae looks at her and says, "Not sure who, but someone took him."

Miss Star looks at her with fear and asks, "What did he look like?"

Rae, trying to help her up, says, "Older, in a black robe."

Miss Star gets moved to a chair with Rae conjuring up a glass of water.

"Was he older or very old," Miss Star asks and takes a drink.

"Not to be rude, but very old. I would guess eighties or so," Rae answers.

"Do you know who that is?" AJ asks.

"Joseph," Miss Star says.

AJ looks at Miss Star confused and asks, "Who is that? How do you know that?"

"Joseph Spawns is the first member of SE. He is not in his eighties. He is over two hundred years old," Miss Star tells them.

Rae starts thinking what she just heard and says, "Wait, Joseph Spawns was killed by his own son because he was on a killing spree."

"No, that's what we were told to help us sleep better. He did step down after killing all but his two youngest children. He has a gift where he can remove his soul from his own body to someone else's. He kills the body while doing it, but he takes their soul to stay alive, taking along with him their power as well," Miss Star tells them.

"So, if he were to take the soul of an elder," Rae asks.

Miss Star thinks about what Jeffrey said as he was dying and says, "We are no longer safe."

"What do we do?" AJ asks.

"We need to get James back," Miss Star says to them.

"Can anyone tell me what is happening?" Rae asks.

Miss Star looks at Rae and explains, "On a nutshell, Joseph is James's grandfather. They have the same power, except James's is one hundred times stronger without trying. If Joseph learns this and takes James' gift, we are all doomed."

"With all due respect, ma'am, how do you know all this?" Rae asks.

Miss Star opens the door, walks inside to get ready, turns her head, and says, "I'm James's aunt."

James wakes up back in the same room. Knowing where he is, he rushes to the door, remembering Benjamin showing him there is no lock. James grabs the handle, trying to pull on it, but it does not budge. James rushes to the window for some kind of peace of mind. James jumps up to look, but the whole thing has been covered. James, feeling confused and lost, leans against the wall with his hand covering his face, sliding into his knees, wondering, *Why now?*

Later that night Miss Star, AJ, Rae, and Mari are in her office, getting everything ready when she gets a message.

"Hey, where you guys at?" Benjamin says to her.

"How dare you even try that?" Miss Star says to him.

"What are you talking about? You said I could meet James tonight," Benjamin says to her.

"Like you don't know what's going on," Miss Star tells him.

"Where you at?" Benjamin asks.

"What does it matter? You got what you wanted," Miss Star says. Out of nowhere Benjamin pops up in her office. Everyone jumps back until Mari recognizes him and puts her hand out, ready for anything.

Miss Star tells her, "Relax, Mari, for now."

"What are you talking about? Where is James?" Benjamin asks.

"You really don't know?" Miss Star says, shocked.

"Know what? You have me very scared right now." Benjamin is feeling worried.

Miss Star looks at him with tears and says, "Your father took him." Benjamin looks down in disbelief and tells Miss Star, "I will get him back. I promise that."

Rae looks at Benjamin and asks, "Excuse me, who are you?

Why has your father, SE founder, taken James and you are here talking about getting him back here"?

Benjamin looks at her and says, "My name is Benjamin. I am James's father, and my father is evil. I have been trying to stop him and his ways for a long time. I'm also Estrella's guardian."

Rae looks at him and says, "Okay."

Mari, looks at him, asking, "Wait, you're his father?"

Benjamin looks at her and says, "Yes, I am, Mari. Mari, as in child of John and Ashley Brush?"

"Yes, why?" Mari asks.

"I have been waiting for you. When the time comes, stay close. We are going to need you," Benjamin tells her.

Mari looks around the room with nobody understanding why.

The next morning James is still leaning on the wall when the door opens. James stands up, trying to see who is there. An older man walks into the room, looking straight at James.

"Hello, can you tell me what is going on? Is Benjamin around?" James asks.

The man lifts his hand, lifting James into the air, frozen in place.

"I am Joseph. You don't need to worry about Benjamin anymore. You will be dealing with me from now on," Joseph tells him.

"You don't understand. Benjamin is my father," James tells Joseph while still frozen in the air.

Joseph looks James in the eyes and tells him, "Oh, Benjamin is your father. That's good to know, because I'm his father."

James, trying to think fast, says to Joseph, "Well, if you're my grandfather, why have me locked up? I can help you."

"That's cute. I have killed my own children for getting in my way. You being my grandson only means you're lucky to be here and alive. Now shut your mouth, and I will let you know when I need you," Joseph tells him while walking out of the room.

James finds himself released from the hold.

Later that day Bob opens the door, bringing a little bit of food for James. James walks to Bob and looks at his face. Bob has bruises all over his face, looking as though he was beaten by someone.

"Bobby, who did this to you?" James asks.

Bob turns to the door, pointing. "Did Joseph do this to you?" James asks.

Bob nods his head with fear and tears in his eyes.

"I need to stop him," James tells him.

Bob shakes his head very fast and hard.

James looks at Bob and tells him, "Bobby, I think I can help. He is my grandfather."

Bob smiles and writes in the dirt on the floor, "F A T H E R."

"He is your father?" James asks.

Bob nods his head with more tears in his eyes.

"That makes you my uncle," James tells him. Bob nods, smiling, looking at James.

"You're my uncle Bobby," James says, trying to make Bob smile again.

Bob turns his head, hearing someone coming. He jumps to his feet, rushing out the door, closing it behind. James can hear what sounds like Joseph close by yelling at Bob, then a large slamming sound a few feet down the wall, followed by sounds of Bob crying in pain. James wants to help, but the door is still locked. James pounds of the door, screaming in anger.

Back on the island Miss Star is trying to figure out how to save James.

Benjamin pops in and tells Miss Star, "They have him in the same place he was before. Now they have stronger magic around it."

"Okay, let's go get him," Miss Star tells him.

"Okay, let's go," AJ tells them while standing with Rae and Mari.

"No, we are going. Not you guys. This is the most dangerous thing any of you will ever do," Miss Star tells them.

"That's why we are going," AJ tells her.

"This is the headquarters for SE, going against the founder who can kill you while being on the other side of a steel door, just knowing you're there," Miss Star tells them.

Mari walks out without saying anything.

"You see, she is being smart about it. You should follow her," Miss Star tells them, but nobody else budges.

Benjamin looks at Miss Star and tells her, "We are all going. We need the help."

Miss Star looks at them all and says, "Okay, let's do this. Use everything you know. Keep your head down and try not to be seen." They are all about to leave when Mari comes back, saying, "Okay, I am ready to go."

They all vanish, popping up in a forest at an outskirt of the land.

Benjamin gets everyone on the land, telling them they need to dress differently. He hands them clothes that his people would wear.

"Where do we change?" Mari asks.

"No need," Benjamin says to them, snapping his fingers.

All the clothes that were in their hands are now what they are wearing and what they were wearing are now in their hands. They put everything in a bag, leaving in a dark place next to the wall and stairs.

Rae looks at the bag and can still see it. She shakes her hand, saying, "Camo."

The bag bends in like nothing is even there.

Benjamin turn to them and tells them, "Okay, follow my lead.

Do not speak out of turn. Do not react to anything you might see. Remember you need to be evil. You do as I say, and we might make it out alive."

"Okay, all we need to do is find James and get out. We can take care of the rest later," Miss Star says.

"AJ, don't try to search for him. This place protects against magic like that," Benjamin tells him.

AJ nods with his heart starting to race.

James, still in the room, hears the door somewhat open. He stands up slowly and walks over to it. James sticks his head out of the door, looking both ways, and can see Bob still lying on the ground. James rushes over to him, checking on him. He has a busted lip, broken nose, his left eye is swollen shut, and maybe some broken ribs.

"Oh, Uncle Bobby, are you okay?" James asks, holding him. Bob looks at James and smiles through the pain.

"Did you open the door for me?" James asks.

Bob smiles, moving his fingers, telling James to run.

James looks at him, telling him, "I'm not going to leave you here. I can't let this happen anymore."

Bob looks at him with tears like he is begging him to go. Bob's eyes suddenly turn wide when James is grabbed by one of the men there. James is taken to Joseph and thrown to his knees.

Joseph, with his back to James, tells him, "I find it interesting how you are my blood. You don't have any of the brains the rest of your family did. You could have ran just now or even tried to kill me while I talk to you right now."

"That is not brains. That is evil. I may have your blood in my veins, but we are nothing alike," James tells him.

Joseph turns around, lifting James to his feet, and tells him, "Now you sound like your father. So pathetic and weak. I should have killed him the same time I killed your mother." James starts to get angry.

Joseph can feel the anger in him and says, "Now that is my grandson. I knew you had it in you. Go ahead hit me with your best shot."

James thinks and tries to calm down, reaching into his pocket, grabbing his charm.

Meanwhile, Benjamin is walking with everyone through the house, making his way to the room where James was. His men walking by look at them like something is off. Benjamin takes them down a winding block staircase, stopping everyone at the bottom.

"Okay, it's right around the corner. Eyes open, everyone," Benjamin tells them.

They turn the corner, and Benjamin finds Bob still on the floor, beaten up.

Benjamin drops down, holding his brother. "Bob, are you okay. Who did this to you?" Benjamin asks.

Bob smiles and points down the hall.

"Was it Father", Benjamin asks? Bob nods in tears.

Benjamin pulls Bob in close, hugging him. "I'm going to take you away from this place," Benjamin tells him. Bob gives him a big smile.

Benjamin tells AJ to look in the room in front of them.

AJ walks to the room and says, "There is nobody in here."

Benjamin asks, "Do you know where James is?"

Bob nods and points to the same place. Benjamin asks Rae to stay with Bob and keep him safe.

Joseph, who is still trying to get James mad enough to hit him, is feeling shocked that he hasn't yet.

"What do you think I did to Bob? We used to call him Robert, until he showed he was useless. That's why he is lying there now. The useless gets beaten. How are you staying to cool right now? Maybe there is something keeping you that way," Joseph says, grabbing the charm out of James's hand, throwing it across the room.

Benjamin, standing right outside the room, watching everything that is happening, fears for James.

As the charm is thrown toward them, Mari leans in, picking it up, and whispers, "Oh no, he can't stay cool without it."

Benjamin looks at Mari and asks, "How bad?"

Mari looks at him and says, "Not sure, but the sun might get jealous of the heat."

Benjamin pulls her in and whispers in her ear.

Joseph looks at James and, in a final attempt to set him off, tells him, "Did you ever hear the story about why your mother left your father. We found him and made him kill or tried to. You see, he wouldn't do it. I saw your mother watching, and I jumped into his body and made it do it."

James is starting to heat up.

"Do you know what the best part was? Because my soul did it. He was still pure at heart and soul, then when he tried to go home after getting away from us, your mother already left, leaving him with nobody. After we found him again on the island, I got to enjoy killing your grandmother and your mother in the same day. Same half hour if you think about it," Joseph says to push him over.

James eyes turn black, and his fire stream, hotter than ever, hits Joseph dead on. After a few seconds, James pulls it back and Joseph is still standing. In shock James's fire dies out fast.

Joseph, dusting himself off, tells James, "Now, I know you're my grandson. One thing you didn't think about. Firestarters can't burn."

Benjamin walks in to stop the madness. "Look at that, you got him," Benjamin says to his father.

"Oh, please, you have been trying to keep me from him," Joseph says to him.

"No, I have been setting this up so you could get what you wanted," Benjamin tells Joseph.

"You forgot one thing. When I used you, I got your gift. I found out everything the last time we met. Nice try, but I already know everything," Joseph tells him.

Mari is sneaking in, going straight to James. Mari hands James his charm. "Here take this," Mari tells James.

Benjamin smiles and says, "Almost everything."

Mari and James take each other's hands. Their charms light up bright while around their necks, and with them mixing their power, they blasted Joseph with everything they have. It is a very hot light blue flame-like energy, a hot-and-cold mix that Joseph couldn't handle. This stream is growing larger and wider than they could have every thought. When they pull back, Joseph is down and almost gone, just clothes wrapping a pile of bones and a little muscle.

Benjamin, feeling justice has been served for his wife, tells everyone,

"We need to get out of here before anyone knows what happened."

They run out of the room, down the hall, grabbing Bob on their way. Then the intruder alarm hits. They all start running even faster, trying to get out safe. Then spells are being thrown from every direction. They are dodging everything coming their way. Miss Star, who is in front of the line, is blocking all big spells. Rae is shooting out spells for defense. Everyone is working together to get everyone safe. They get outside where the SE men are trying to block them from leaving. Miss Star rises up herself into the air with her hand motioning everything in their way to split, holding them in place, unable to move. They all head back to the outskirt by the trees and vanish back to the island.

CHAPTER

FAMILY STRONG

They all make it back home. Miss Star looks around, checking heads, adding two more. All six of them are standing in front of the Main Building. They all stop in their tracks, listening for any sound or alarm. After a good minute has passed, they all look around at each other faces almost in shock. One by one they start smiling and cheering.

"We made it. We made it," they start chanting, hugging each

other, jumping around, not realizing that it is still the middle of the night.

Miss Star tells everyone to move to her office.

They walk down the hall to Miss Stars's office. Benjamin is helping Bob walk down the hall as he is looking at how much has changed. They get close to her office when Benjamin asks, "Estrella, where is this office? I don't see anything with your name."

"Right here," Miss Star says as they all pop in in her office.

Benjamin sits Bob in a chair at her desk. He turns to looks back and can see the slot, nodding with a smile. Miss Star pulls out the first aid kit to clean up Bob. Benjamin takes to kit with James, offering to help. Bob, seeing his family helping him, gives a very large smile.

"Excuse me, I am sorry to ask. But why can Bob not speak?" Mari asks.

"No, you're good. Bob can't speak because when he was little, he was trying to learn spells. He couldn't say any correctly. For anyone who don't speak clearly, the magic does something else. In this case, Bob was trying to lift a chair, ended up conjuring up snow over our father's head. Our father got mad and made sure he could never say another spell again by hitting him in the face and neck with one," Benjamin tells her. "Has anyone ever tried to fix it?" Rae asks.

"It was forbidden. Any magic he did couldn't be undone," Benjamin tells them.

Rae looks at Bob, telling him, "I will do my best to try and fix you." Bob smiles, shaking her hand.

"Mr. Ben, I was also wondering how you knew what would happen if James and I used our gift together?" Mari asks.

James head and ears perk up almost like a dog getting called.

"That is a whole new story," Benjamin tells her.

"After everything that we just went through, I am sure we have gotten to that point," Mari states to him.

Benjamin smiles at her, saying, "You're right, but this need to go back to the start of everything. I mean, back to the beginning."

Miss Star looks at Benjamin and tells him, "Only if you think they're ready. Make sure to keep it honest."

"That is the only way I know how to do it," Benjamin tells Miss Star.

Benjamin tells them to all to sit down, and he begins telling them the story.

"This all starts twenty years ago. James, before you were born, it was said there was a prophecy about a child that would burn the world down as it stands. Most people thought of you because of who your mother and I were. My bloodline, the evilest, and your mother, being pure good. We left this place to hide. You see SE has known where this place is but couldn't get in. We left with no way to track us. Mari, your parents were some of our best friends. They came right after you were born. There was a prophecy about a child who was cold that would freeze the greatest evil in the world. Now, to have child that would freeze and that being the only thing that can stop a firestarter, then a child born frozen and living meant you needed to be moved. One night we made charms using your gifts to help you. One for freeze and one for fire. If you use your charm made by the other gift, your gift is dormant. However, use the one for you, your gift is a hundred times stronger. When you two were babies, right before you had your charms, James took your hand. The power we saw from that was the most incredible thing anyone ever saw. You two hit a tree with it, and the place where you two hit, the tree was heated cold. I thought it couldn't hurt to try."

"Are you saying you did not know for sure?" Mari asks.

"I wasn't sure," Benjamin tells her. Mari nods, thanking him.

"I have a question. Why did you break into the island with SE?" James asks.

"Truth, I heard my son was here. I was hoping to see him. When one of the men hit you with that spell and I saw you, all I wanted to do was stop and help but that would have been obvious. I didn't want to blow any cover or put you at risk," Benjamin tells James.

"Why did Jeffrey take James to you?" AJ asks.

"Jeffrey knew he was my son and came to me. He said, 'We have your son, and I don't want him here.' Basically, he did not like the fact James is that strong. It scared him, and he did not like the fear," Benjamin tells AJ.

After a few hours talking about things that happened and catching up, they see the sun is starting to rise. Phoebe flies into the window, appearing to be worried.

"Where have you guys been?" Phoebe asks.

"I'm sorry, I should have told you. We had to take care of something. Now everything is okay. No need to worry," Miss Star tells her.

Phoebe looks around at everyone in the room. "Why do we have Benjamin and Bob here? What happened?"

Benjamin stands up, looking at her, asking, "Who are you? Do I know you?"

Phoebe smiles at him and turns to Miss Star, asking again more sternly, "What happened?"

"James was taken by Joseph. We went to SE headquarters, got him back. In the process James and Mari mixed their power and destroyed him," Miss Star tells her.

"No, there is nothing that can destroy him," Phoebe tells her.

"All that was left was clothes bones and maybe a little muscle," Miss Star tells her.

"Then he is not dead, just down and weak. He will be back. He always comes back," Phoebe tells them.

Benjamin starts asking again. "Who are you? Why do you think this?"

Phoebe looks him in the eyes. "Do you really not know?"

Benjamin jumps back like he is seeing a ghost, saying, "It can't be.

I watched you…I watched you…"

"You think you did," Phoebe says.

"How is this possible?" Benjamin asks.

"What is going on here?" James asks.

Miss Star looks at James and asks, "James, what do you know about Phoebe?"

"Nothing other than she grows fast and she is your daughter," James replies.

Miss Star smiles and tells him, "No, she is not my child. I take care of her and raise her. Phoebe is my grandmother."

"I'm a phoenix. Anytime I die for any reason, I come back through the ashes," Phoebe tells them. "When your father killed me that day, I was reborn through the ashes. Estrella has been raising me until I am full grown again. Then I can take my place here again."

James, in shock of what he just heard, asks, "That would make you my…"

"Great-grandmother," Phoebe tells him.

"You are here on this island because…" James asks.

Phoebe looks at him with her hand on his shoulder and says,

"Because I started this place. I once knew Joseph. He has always been evil. Knowing everything he wanted to do, I brought all who would want to join me here. I put the shield on. I made sure we were all safe. Then somehow it was said MEMPA was here and SE broke in, thanks to Jeffrey. Now I will redo everything even stronger than before."

Phoebe walks over to Bob and Benjamin, telling them, "I know what you did. You are both good souls. I will make sure you have a home here. Please give all the same respect that you would give me." Bob smiles, nodding his head.

"Now I know what today is. Everyone, go to your home, get cleaned up, and we will meet you at breakfast," Phoebe tells them.

"You still do that?" Benjamin asks.

"Still baby, I never stopped," Phoebe says with a smile as she turns back into a phoenix, flying out of the window.

"You heard her," Miss Star tells them.

A little while later they meet up at the breakfast table. Benjamin and Bob walk side by side with James and David. David feeling happiness he didn't know until after everything was done and they all came back safe. James and family move to sit down at the table when Miss Star calls them all over to sit with her. Mari walks up to the table with her aunt Fran, who feels the same way as David, and Rae with Miss Star calls her to the same place.

James, looks at the table, saying, "I don't think there is enough space for all of us here."

Miss Star stands up, lifts her arms in front of herself, rubbing her hands together. The table starts moving, extending itself to make more room. "Do you think that is enough room?" Miss Star asks.

James, feeling surprised, smiles at Miss Star. Phoebe stands up, holding her glass, asks for everyone's attention.

"I know we do this breakfast thing because I asked for this a long time ago. You all know you have a choice to be here. For you that are here, I thank you all. I wanted to say a few words about two new people here today, Benjamin and Bob. I pray you will all treat them with the same respect you do for me. They are a part of my family. Being family, I would like to say, I welcome you both. If you need anything, please do not hesitate," Phoebe tells them with a very large smile. Everyone lifts their glass to that.

After the meal Rae walks up to Bob, telling him, "I think I might have figured out a way to help."

Bob, Benjamin, and James follow Rae. David looks on, almost feeling left out. The four of them arrive at a house.

"Is this where you live?" James asks.

Rae turns her head, telling him, "Yeah, it not much, but it's all mine. When my parents were killed, this is what I got."

James, with a look of putting his foot in his mouth, apologizes.

"Don't worry about it. There is no way you could have ever known," Rae tells him.

"May I ask how they died?" James asks.

Rae, gathering everything she is about to use, tells him, "Well, from my understanding, they left the island for something and were caught in some kind of cross fire. I don't know much, but I guess they popped up in a building as it was being destroyed. Bomb went off, and they never had a chance. My mom was my dad's guardian. She never saw it coming. They loved to go to a place inside that building not knowing what was going to happen."

"I am so sorry," James says to her, grabbing her hand.

"Thank you, but I'm fine, really. I was a long time ago," Rae tells him.

Rae tells Bob to have a seat in a chair. Bob sits down, feeling a little fear. Rae looks at Bob and tells him, "You said no one was allowed to undo any magic Joseph did, right?"

Benjamin looks at Rae with a curious look, saying, "Yeah, if anyone tried, then you would be killed."

"Okay, good, I would like to try something if that is okay with you, Bob. This might hurt though," Rae tells him. Bob nods his head in fear.

Rae turns around, grabbing a glass, handing it to Bob. "Please, drink every drop of this," Rae tells him. Bob looks at Benjamin. Benjamin nods, smiling back at him.

Bob takes a deal breath and shoots the liquid down his throat as fast as he can.

Rae looks at Bob closely, asking, "How do you feel?" Bob shrugs his shoulders.

"Try to say something," Rae tells Bob.

"Like what?" Bob says.

Everyone in the room smiles, hearing Bob's voice. Benjamin starts to cry. Bob jump up in disbelief that he is talking. "How did you…? Thank you, thank you," Bob says to Rae, crying, hugging her tight.

Later that evening James is walking with Benjamin by the lake. Nothing much is being said, just walking, looking at the water and the stars.

Benjamin looks at James and says to him, "They say a man who spends him time looking at the water and stars without a word has a lot on his mind."

James takes a deep breath and says, "I know I should be happy. I should be on top of the world. I have my father and uncle that I didn't know I had in my life. I don't need to stress on anything big anymore, but something just doesn't feel right."

"What do you mean?" Benjamin asks.

"I have these dreams. I have had them for a long time," James tells him.

Benjamin sits James down in the sand and asks, "How long?"

James looks at Benjamin with fear on him face. "Ever since I can remember. Five years old, I think."

Benjamin thinks, *That's a long time.*

James can see the look and asks, "What is the look for?"

"I'm sorry, I was thinking, that is a long time," Benjamin tells him.

James's head drops down between his legs.

Benjamin can see the stress on his shoulders and asks, "What is happening in these dreams?"

"Well, in the dreams everything is on fire. I hear people screaming my name. Not until I got here, did I start seeing faces," James tells Benjamin.

"Like who?" Benjamin asks.

James looks into the water and says, "Mari, Fran, David, even Miss—I mean, Aunt Estrella—and you."

"Are you hurting anyone of us?" Benjamin asks.

James looks at him with tears in his eyes, saying, "That's the thing. I don't know. I know the fire is coming from me. I don't want to hurt anyone." James starts crying.

Then Benjamin, lifting to his knees, quickly wraps his arm around James. "You will not hurt anyone unless they are bad and are trying to hurt you or our family. Do you hear me?" Benjamin tells James, wiping the tears from James's face. James nods, smiling.

They both rise to their feet. Then Benjamin stops in his tracks, saying, "Oh no, we need to go."

"Wait, what? Where do we need to go?" James asks.

"I can't tell you, I promised," Benjamin tells him.

"Now you need to," James tells him. James is standing in place with his arms crossed.

Benjamin looks at him and smiles, saying, "You are just like your mother. Knowing you will not move unless I say please don't say anything."

James nods his head with a smile.

"Everyone is setting up a special dinner for us. Being a family again and all," Benjamin tells him.

James smiles and says, "Now, was that so hard?"

Benjamin gives him a look, putting his arm around James. They both walk to James's home.

They get to James's, and Benjamin pulls James in close, whispering, "I didn't say anything."

"Okay, I know nothing," James responds.

James opens the door with no light or anything inside. James turns on a light; and everyone—David, AJ, Rae, Mari, Fran, Bob, and Miss Star—got out, shouting, "HAPPY BIRTHDAY!"

Much like Mari, James forgot it was his birthday. The house was filled with balloons and ribbons everywhere. James thanks everyone.

Miss Star walks up to James, asking, "After everything, you have your family all here for you on your birthday, how does it feel?"

James, unsure what to say, responds with "Great." Then James looks to his room where he can see a woman standing and asks, "Who is that over there in my room?"

Everyone turns their head to his room, not seeing anything.

"James, there is nobody there," Miss Star tells him.

James puts his drink down, looking and walking over to the darkened room, still seeing the image of what looks to be a woman. James turns on a light, and the image disappears.

James looks back at everyone, saying, "None of you saw her?" AJ closes his eyes to see what James saw.

"No, I'm sorry," David tells him.

AJ stands up, telling James, "I know what you saw. I just don't know who it was."

"What did she look like?" Benjamin asks.

"You know that picture Miss Star has in her office on top of her bookcase?" AJ asks.

"The one of two teen girls standing on an old porch," Benjamin responds.

"Yes, he saw one of the girls," AJ tells them. MissStar puts her hands on her face.

"Do you know who that is a picture of?" Benjamin asks.

"No, I can't say I do," AJ responds.

"That is a picture of Estrella and Marcelina, James's mother," Benjamin tells him.

Miss Star asks James, "Are you sure?"

"Yes, she was here. She was also in my dream. Back when I got hurt. She came to me, telling me to come back. She said there is more to do," James responds.

Silence falls over the room.

Out of nowhere James says, "At least my mom saw me on my birthday."

Miss Star, knowing what James is doing, says, "Happy birthday, James."

The night continues as planned with the thought of Marcelina still in their minds. James is enjoying his family and friends. He walks into the kitchen to help Mari with dishes when she tells him to stop.

"What?" James asks.

"When it was for me, you did the dishes. Now it is my turn," Mari tells him.

James smiles, telling her, "Yeah, but you didn't listen then, why should I listen now?"

Mari smiles back, knowing it was true.

After dishes are finished, they both sit down at the table and Mari asks, "Do you remember what we had talked about that night?"

James smiles. "How could I forget?"

Mari takes James's hand, asking, "What do you think? Do we know enough yet?"

James turns his head toward their families, responding, "I think so." Mari and James lean in for a kiss.

"Mari, are you guys ready?" Fran asks. Mari and James stop in their tracks.

"Yes, if you are," Mari responds.

They both stand up as James follows them to the door, walking them out. James hugs Mari, closing the door behind her. Seconds later there is a knock at the door. James opens the door, and Mari is standing there, looking at him.

"Did you forget something?" James asks.

"Yes, I did," Mari responds, giving James a big kiss. "I have been wanting that for a long time."

James is still standing there with a smile and no words. Benjamin, Bob, and David were all standing there, staring at James proudly.

"Have a good night," Mari says to James.

James smiles, waving, saying, "Yeah, you night good too."

Mari smiles, walking away, knowing she left him tongue tied.

James closes the door still wearing a smile. He can see everyone looking at him.

"What are you guys looking at?" James asks.

They all turn their heads. James walks by all of them, going into his room. James lies on his bed with his arms behind his head, feeling happy for what finally happened but wondering why his mother keeps popping up like that. Something isn't making sense. When he saw Eugene, it was clear, but he can't see his mother like that. Something is off or wrong. James closes his eyes, hoping in the morning something will come to him.

The next morning James is at the library looking for anything kind of information about different plane or spiritual planes. James isn't seeing much. Rae walks up.

"Hey, kid, how you doing?"

"Hi, James, how is your day going?" Rae asks.

"I'm good. I need your help real fast," James says to her.

Rae takes off her glasses, asking, "What do you need?"

"I was looking for something of different planes and can't find much. Is there anything more you might know," James asks.

"Is this about last night?" Rae asks.

"Yes, I was thinking about things. I can see spirits like I see you, but I can't see my mother like that. What if she is stuck somewhere and is asking for help?"

Rae nods her head, agreeing with him. "If that is true, there is nothing here I would have that you have not seen. All these books are on things that have been shown or proven," Rae tells him.

"Then tell me why you have book about MEMPA if nobody knows what it is?" James asks.

"They mention it, but as you said, nobody knows what it is," Rae tells him.

James turns around in frustration, saying, "I'm sorry. I'm just trying to understand what is happening."

Rae looks at him, saying, "I get it. Let me look into some things, and I will see what I can find."

James gives her a hug, thanking her.

"Now go relax. Enjoy your time off," Rae tells him.

James walks away, agreeing with her, but with no intentions of relaxing. James leaves the library heading straight to see his aunt. He runs into her outside the library.

"Hey, I was just on my way to see you," James says to Miss Star.

"What can I do for you?" Miss Star asks him.

"I was thinking about last night, and I was wondering if you might know anything about other planes," James asks.

"James, I understand where you are coming from. If I could get my sister back, I would have already done it. I watched her die, and you saw her spirit, that's all. There is no way we can get her back," Miss Star tells him.

James feeling shut down tells her, "No, what I saw was not a spirit. That was something else. I think that if we could—"

"STOP! I don't want to hear any more about this," Miss Star tells him.

James walks away without another word.

James goes to see AJ feeling like nobody wants to help. James finds AJ working outside his home.

AJ walks up to him, saying, "Bro, let's go inside."

They both walk inside where AJ tries to help James think about what is happening.

"Do you really think that she might lost somewhere in another place," AJ asks.

"I don't know, maybe. I just need to find out what is all out there," James says as he sits back in the chair.

AJ can feel what is on James mind. AJ looks at him and says, "Let's find out everything we can on different plane first. I'm with you until the end."

James smiles, saying, "I knew you would be."

AJ goes around asking everyone about it. Not many people will say anything. AJ starts to feel like that it is something that no one wants to talk about.

James goes to his father to ask him. James gets to Benjamin's home, knocking on the door.

Bob open the door, "James, how is my favorite nephew?"

"I'm okay. Is Benjamin here?" James asks.

"Yes, he is. He is in the back. You know if you called him dad, he would love that," Bob tells him.

"Okay, thanks," James says to Bob, walking to the back. James can see Benjamin through the crack in the doorway.

He knocks on the door, pushing it open, sticking his head through. "Hey, Ben, how you doing?"

"Hey, please come in. What can I do for you?" Benjamin asks.

James looks around the room, seeing how well Benjamin has adapted to his new life.

"I have a question. I need to know everything you know," James asks.

"Okay, sure," Benjamin says to him, wondering what it could be.

"Everyone has run me out for asking," James tells him.

"Ask away," Benjamin tells him.

"What do you know but different spiritual plane?" James asks.

Benjamin turns his head, "That's what you want to know? Man, you put me in a touchy place."

"What do you mean?" James asks.

"That is something no one talks about. Why do you want to know? Wait, is this because of last night?" Benjamin asks.

"Yes, I think Mom is stuck somewhere, and I want to help her," James tells him.

Benjamin takes a deep breath, not wanting to say no but can't really tell him.

James looks at him with an almost begging look. "Please, Dad."

Benjamin, finally hearing that word, can't help but say, "Okay."

Benjamin closes the door and sits down.

"James, you need to understand that what you are saying is not to be known," Benjamin tells him.

"I am getting that. Why is that?" James asks.

"That's just the way it is. The plane you are asking about is not in any book. This is something that no one should know about. Only a few people have even asked about it," Benjamin tells him.

"Then how do you know about it?" James asks.

"You have AJ asking around, huh?" Benjamin asks. James nods.

"I did the same thing with your mother. She saw something," Benjamin tells him. "What happened?" James asks.

"Same thing. Until one guy named Eugene told me about it. He said there is another plane on this island. Few know, but if you are killed by magic on this island, your soul gets placed there," Benjamin tells him.

"Why does nobody want to talk about this?" James asks.

"Because this plane is the same plane that Joseph's soul came from. This is why everything was made to stop him. However, that is the one place we can't touch," Benjamin tells him.

"The fear of him is why nothing gets said," James asks.

"Yes," Benjamin responds.

James stands up, asking, "Is there any way to get to it?"

"Not to my knowledge, why?" Benjamin asks.

"I'm going to save my mother," James tells him.

CHAPTER

NEW FEARS

A group of people are standing in a circle. Everything seems to be moving in slow motion. A man throws a green light at a light-blue light. Th e light is steady on each other, pushing back and forth. Th e group of people are screaming, "JJJAAAAAMMMMEEESSSSS!"

Mari is lying on the ground next to James. Everyone is trying to help, but no one can get near the fight, like they are stuck looking in a bubble.

Then the green flashes brightly, and James wakes up in a cold sweat. James rolls to the side of bed, sitting up, wiping the sweat off his face. *These dreams are becoming too much*, James thinks.

He stands up, getting ready for the day, opening his curtains, the warm sun shining on his face. He walks out of his bedroom room with a good morning to his godfather. Walking into the kitchen to eat, James enjoys his breakfast. Telling David, he will see him later, James walks out of the house into a dark place that is as though the sun burned out. James is no longer on the island. He is helping people get to safety. There are all types of creatures destroying homes. James comes face to-face with two different creatures at the same time—a Harpy (part eagle, part-human) and a Cerberus (three-headed dog). He tries to hit them with a stream of fire. Nothing is coming out. James, scared, starts to run. Immediately, he is grabbed by the Harpy, lifting into the air, dropping his straight into the mouth of the Cerberus's middle head.

James jumps out of bed. Looking around at everything, James can see it is the middle of the night. James walks around the house to make sure everything is back to normal. Realizing that it was all a dream, James returns to his bed. Unable to get back to sleep, he decides to lie there.

A little later in the day, Benjamin goes to Rae's house, catching her before she left. "Morning, Rae," Benjamin greets her.

"Good morning, Benjamin. Not trying to be rude, but I'm on my way to the library. Is there anything I can do for you?" Rae asks.

"No, but there is something I can do for you," Benjamin tells her.

Rae turns her head, asking, "What do you mean?"

"May I ask you some questions about your parents?" Benjamin asks.

"What do you mean, my parents?" Rae asks.

"I might have known them," Benjamin tells her.

Rae quickly walks off, saying, "We will talk later."

Later that evening Benjamin is still at Rae's house. Rae is walking up to the house and sees that Benjamin is there.

"You have good timing. How did you know I would be home right now?" Rae asks.

Benjamin stands up, saying, "I didn't. I have been here waiting the whole time. I didn't want to miss you."

Rae walks to her front door. "Why is this so important to you?" Rae asks, opening the door, waving Benjamin to come in.

"I just need to know something. If the answer is not what I think, I will drop it," Benjamin tells her while she is in another room making something.

Rae comes back with coffee. "Okay, ask me."

Benjamin takes the coffee, asking, "Were your parents' names Nicholas and Elizabeth?"

"Well, yeah, but you could have found that out from anyone," Rae tells him.

"You're right. What do you know about where they were from? Did they ever talk about any family cousins or anything?" Benjamin asks.

"Are you sure they did?" Rae tells him.

Benjamin stands up and asks, "Are there any picture of family?

The only one I see is of you and your parents," Benjamin tells her.

"What is your point?" Rae asks.

Benjamin grabs the picture, looking at it, saying, "I knew your father very well."

"How well?" Rae asks.

"A long time ago your father came here looking to get away from everything he saw. Your father showed

me how to do magic. I remember the day he left. He said he met a girl and was going with her, somewhere safe. He told me that he would come back for me. When I saw him again, it was like nothing changed. He saw me, and we were close again. Nicolas and Elizabeth survived the war helping everyone. Some years later, after you were born, they were told to end all hiding, to meet at a building where they first met. That is why that place was so special. They went, and the building was destroyed. I tried to warn them about what was about to happen, but I wasn't fast enough to get to them. Joseph destroyed the building to get rid of what he did," Benjamin tells her.

"Why are you telling me this?" Rae asks with tears in her eyes.

"I needed you to know the truth. I know because your father made me promise to look after you if anything ever happens," Benjamin tells her.

"Why you?" Rae asks.

Benjamin looks at Rae's eyes, saying, "His exact last words to me were, 'If anything happens to me. Please watch over your niece.' Then I replied, 'Anything for you, big brother.'"

Later that night Benjamin is walking home when he finds James walking outside by himself.

"James, what are you doing out here?" Benjamin calls out.

James doesn't answer, continuing to walk around. Benjamin walks up to James, seeing his eyes open without any kind of acknowledgement for anything around him. Benjamin, unsure of what is going on, tries again to get James attention by standing in front of him. James does not stop but tries to walk through him.

Miss Star pops up, telling Benjamin, "I heard you what is going on."

Benjamin points to James, saying, "I'm not sure what he is doing. I have tried to talk to him, and he keeps going like he is—"

"Sleepwalking," Miss Star says.

Out of nowhere AJ is running up like he knows something is wrong. AJ walks up to James, saying, "We should be fine as long as he is wearing his charm."

"Is he?" Miss Star asks.

"Yes, we are okay," AJ tells her.

James gets into a fighting position when Benjamin walks up to him, grabbing his shoulders, shouting, "JAMES, WAKE UP."

"Ben, stop doing that. That could make him worse," Miss Star tells him.

Benjamin quickly stops the shouting.

James suddenly screams, "NO, I will never stop. I will never let you hurt them. You will have to go through me."

AJ shouts, "Stop him."

James grabs his charm, ripping it off himself, bursting into a flame. Everyone steps back, not to get burned. Mari comes out of nowhere, grabbing the charm from the ground, jumping into action, placing her cold hands on his chest.

James drops down, body and fire. James is lying on the ground, eyes closed, with Benjamin standing back as Miss Star and AJ check on him. Mari puts the charm necklace back on James.

Miss Star asks Mari and AJ, "What is going on? Does he normally sleepwalk?"

AJ says, "No, this is a first. He has been having some really bad nightmares."

"Like what?"

"Something about fighting. People dying all around him. He has been trying to protect everyone. He has also been trying to find out about different planes," AJ tells them.

"He asked me about it. I wouldn't tell him anything," Miss Star explains.

Benjamin closes his eyes, telling them, "I told him about the planes. Before you say anything, when he asked me, he said, 'Please, Dad,' and well…"

James starts to wake up with Mari still holding him.

"Mari, hi. What are you doing?" James starts looking around.

"Where am I at?" James asks.

Benjamin moves to help him to his feet. "Well, my son, you were sleepwalking and tried to fight something."

James eyes turn wide. "I didn't hurt…?"

"No, you didn't hurt anyone. Mari made sure of that," AJ tells him.

James looks around at everyone, asking, "Why is everyone out here?"

AJ and Mari both say, "Had a bad feeling."

Miss Star tells them, "Benjamin called for me telepathically."

They all look at Benjamin. "What, oh, I was on my way home after talking to someone," Benjamin tells them.

Mari and AJ take James back to him home, where they decide to stay with him for everyone's safety.

David walks out of his room, looking at the three people sleeping on the couch. David smiles, continuing with what he is doing. He walks into the kitchen, making coffee, being as loud as he can to wake them all up. By the third clank, they all wake up.

David, looking at them and trying not to laugh, says, "Oh sorry, I didn't mean to wake you all up."

The three stretch out, waking up, when David asks, "Another long night?"

"You could say that. James was found sleepwalking outside," AJ tells him.

David spits out his coffee, rushing into the room. "What do you mean, sleepwalking?"

James looks at David, telling him, "Don't worry, I was found fast and they stayed here to make sure it didn't happen again."

"Okay, next time let me know what is happening," David tells them.

"Okay, we will," they tell David.

Later that day James and his friends are being called to Miss Star's office. They get to her slot, but no one was there, just a note. The note only says a few things, "Fresno, CA, Harpy," and "Please clean up mess." AJ looks at the note, telling Mari and James, "Okay, let's get ready." They walk outside with James, asking, "What are these things?"

"We will be there in a minute. Just be careful. I don't think this will be easy," AJ tells them.

"Why is that?" Mari asks.

AJ points to the name, saying, "These things fly."

AJ takes their hands, teleporting from the island to Fresno, California. They get there and are standing in a wooded park with trees all around a grass field.

"What are we looking for again?" Mari asks.

AJ point up in the air, shouting, "THAT!"

They all duck as the Harpy flies over them like they are attacking. "What the—" James asks.

"Harpy, very deadly and hard to kill," AJ tells him.

"If one is hard to kill, how hard would that be?" James asks, looking to the distance in front of them.

There look to be at least four Harpies. They rush under a gazebo to try and not be seen until they can plan.

"I think we should get them all to one place and freeze some and burn some," Mari tells them.

James hears something behind them. He moves closer to see what it could be.

"JAMES!", Mari calls out.

"Sorry, I thought I heard something," James replies. Mari starts talking again.

James hears the sound again. "I think there is something in there," James tells them.

"Unless it is going to try and eat us, I'm not worried," AJ tells him.

James looks even closer, then a Cerberus jump out from the bushes. Everyone jumps back with James standing in front of them, remembering his dreams.

James whispers, "Can I burn them?"

"No, not without hurting anyone near," AJ replies still in a whisper.

"What do we do?" James asks in a whisper.

"Let me think," AJ says in a whisper.

"Are you guys kidding me?" Mari says.

She stands in front of them, clapping her hands together three times, saying, "Música."

Next thing they see is the Cerberus starting to drop down with its eyes closing.

"What was that?" James asks.

Mari backs at him, almost laughing, "You did not pay much attention to the books. A Cerberus falls asleep to music. I just made music play in its head."

"That was smart, but how do we stop the Harpies," James asks.

AJ thinks and says, "What if we got them close enough and freeze them?"

They all run to the middle of the field, calling out to the Harpies, trying to get their attention. All four Harpies start flying toward them.

"I hope this works," Mari tells them.

James, Mari, and AJ are standing back-to-back to make sure there are no surprises. The Harpies are right above them when Mari puts her hands up, shouting, "FREEZE!"

All the Harpies freeze and drop out of the air like a bag of rocks, hitting the ground solid.

"You did it," James tells Mari, feeling exited.

"Can we go back home now?" Mari asks.

AJ looks at her, saying, "Sure, all we need to do is grab all of these creatures back with us, to make sure nobody gets hurt."

They start trying to grab the Harpy one at a time. Mari looks at a Harpy and tells AJ, "I do not think they are dead. This one is still moving inside the ice."

James takes off his charm, saying, "Back up, everyone. I'll light them up."

AJ jumps in, telling James, "NO! We can't do that. If freezing didn't work, fire will only make it worse."

"Then what do we do?" James asks.

AJ, not sure, tells them, "Let's take them back to the island. Miss Star will know what to do."

Quickly they move all the Harpies and the Cerberus back to the island. They make sure they're all in a place that is locked away in a prison-type place hidden in a mountainside of the island that is called the Cage.

They walk down to Miss Star's office, which is still empty. Unsure of what to do, they decide to wait for her until she comes back. After a few hours of waiting, they start to get impatient.

"Where is she?" James says, pacing in a circle.

"Relax, James. I'm sure she is very busy doing whatever she does," AJ tells him.

"I'm going to check outside again, see if she is coming," James tells AJ while walking down the hall to the outside.

James steps out, looking around at everyone, hoping to find Miss Star without luck. James looks toward the mountainside cage where they put the creatures, and he notices that smoke is coming from where they are at.

James runs inside, telling James and Mari there is smoke coming from the cage. They all go outside, looking at the problem.

"We need to get there fast," Mari tells them.

"I have an idea. Follow me," James tells them while rushing to his home.

He runs to the backyard and pulls a large tarp off a covered item.

James smiles and says, "I think this might help."

AJ looks at the car, telling James, "I really thought I would never see this car again. She is a beauty. Okay, let's go."

They all get into the car heading straight to the cage.

They rush up the mountainside, with James enjoying being behind the wheel again. They arrive to the cage and see that the smoke is coming from the top. They rush inside the building and find that all the creatures are not frozen anymore. They are trying to destroy the cage in order to get out. The smoke is from a small fire from electric wires being torn, burning the top wood panels. All the Harpies fly over their heads and out of the building.

Chasing them out, James, Mari, and AJ are not sure what to do. James turns around to make sure the Cerberus is still inside, and it is. The Harpies turn around, heading toward the cage, attacking those who brought them there.

Flying straight at them with razor-sharp claws from their feet, out ready for killing, the first one is seconds away from James when it folds up hitting the ground hard and fast.

"What the hell is going on? I leave your side from a minute, and this happens," Benjamin says to James, throwing him a crossbow.

"How did you know we needed help?" James asks.

"First shoot and try not to miss. Next, you're my son. I know when something is going on. Plus, I saw you driving here, and there is only one reason you would be driving. Something happened, and you need to move fast," Benjamin tells James.

James is shooting, but it looks like nothing is working. "Why will they not stay down?" James asks.

Benjamin looks at him, shouting, "Aim for the chest. Right in the middle. You have to hit their heart. The silver in their heart is the only way to kill them."

Benjamin shoots down two more. James moves to shoot the last one when it drops out of sight. James walks to the edge of the cliff, looking down, trying to see where the Harpy might be at. The coast is completely clear.

James turns his head, saying, "There is nothing here."

The all drop down low to make sure there are no surprises. Everyone is looking to the side and the sky. All sound seems to have stopped. Then out of nowhere the Cerberus bursts out of the doorway, giving out a loud howl with all three heads. AJ and Mari stand in place, trying not to move. Benjamin is standing in place with shock written on his face. Then the Harpy swoops down, trying hit AJ or Mari.

The Cerberus catches the Harpy with one head on the head, another head on the torso/wings, and the last head, grabbing the waist, all pulling different directions at the same time.

Following the eating of the Harpy, James, looking at this, says to Benjamin, "I think we just found another way to kill the Harpies."

Benjamin nods his head, agreeing with that comment.

Benjamin looks at the Cerberus, asking, "Where did this come from?"

"We brought it back from the same place as the Harpies," AJ tells him.

"Why were you there?" Benjamin asks.

"Miss Star asked us to go clean up a mess, and we had no idea how to stop them. We brought them back in hope Miss Star could tell us what to do," Mari tells him.

"Why would she send you without telling you how to stop them?" Benjamin asks.

The three looks at each other, shaking their heads. Mari hands Benjamin the note.

Benjamin closes his eyes, trying to talk to Miss Star. "Estrella, where are you?" Benjamin asks.

"Not now," Miss Star replies.

"I need to talk to you right now," Benjamin tells her.

"Not a good time. I am busy," Miss Star tells him.

"Fine, tell me why you sent James, Mari and AJ to get Harpies without telling them how to stop them," Benjamin asks.

"I didn't," Miss Star tells him.

"I am looking at the note," Benjamin tells her.

"I'll be there soon," Miss Star tells him.

Benjamin opens his eyes, telling James and friends, "She says she didn't leave any note."

Unsure of what that means, nobody says a word.

The Cerberus rubs one of its heads against Mari. Mari, scared, puts her hand on its head, petting it. The Cerberus loves it.

"I think you should keep it. It seems to like you," Benjamin tells Mari.

The Cerberus growls at him.

Mari looks under the Cerberus, saying, "Not it. He likes me."

The Cerberus leans into her, and she says, "What should I name you?"

The Cerberus starts moving around with excitement like it understood her.

"How about Lucky?" Mari says while Lucky is moving around with excitement even more.

"Why lucky?" AJ asks.

Mari looks at AJ, saying, "The fact that you are lucky he did not eat you."

Everyone starts to laugh. "Okay, that works. Let's get back," James tells them.

They all get in the car, except Mari, who Lucky made her get on his back. As they go through town, everyone is scared seeing Lucky with James driving in front of them. They park the car back where it was and walk to the Main Building to wait for Miss Star to return.

They walk up to the Main Building with perfect timing. Miss Star runs into them at the entrance.

Miss Star, with a look of shock at finding Mari riding a Cerberus, asks, "Do I want to know?"

"The job we thought you sent us on, we found him. I put him to sleep, and we brought Lucky and four Harpies back with us, unsure what to do. We found out…" Mari starts explaining.

"I just meant the Cerberus. Did you call him Lucky?" Miss Star asks.

"Yes, he helped us and took a liking to me. I named him Lucky. As long as it is okay, can I keep him?" Mari asks.

"Yes, that is fine. However, he is your responsibility," Miss Star tell her.

"Yes, ma'am," Mari responds.

"The note," Miss Star asks. Benjamin hands it to her.

Miss Star looks at it for a second, then says, "I can see why you thought it was me. Someone really wanted you to think so. I never wrote this. I have not been here for some time. I left after you two got James home. I went to someone to find out why everything is happening to him."

James jumps up, asking, "Well, what can we do? Can I help her?"

Miss Star starts to tear up, saying, "I was told that if you go there, you will never be able to make it back. If you go, that will be killing you."

James, in disbelief, says, "How is that? Joseph is from there. He used it."

Miss Star, understanding the frustration, tells him, "I know.

That is because he uses the body. He was never attached to one. The body you saw is one he used. Plus, that was his gift. I'm so sorry, James."

James, very upset with the news, walks away. AJ follows, trying to talk to him without luck. Mari tries talking to him as well with no luck. James walks away from everyone, not wanting to hear anymore.

CHAPTER

HOW IT STARTED

Children around eleven years old are playing in a beautiful forest. There is a small creek with fresh water running through. Several little girls and boys are laughing, playing by the small bridge that was put there by the kids. The small houses are close together, each one the size of a studio apartment. Th e mothers of the children are outside doing their daily chores.

Two little girls, one with blonde hair and brown eyes and the other with white-reddish mix hair and gray eyes, are coming down the mountainside near the homes. One little girl is losing control and is about to run straight into a wall when the second girl feels her fear.

She lifts her hand, shouting, "HALT."

The first girl stops centimeters from a face-plant along the wall.

Then a woman calls out, "Phoebe."

The second girl replies, "Coming, Mommy."

Phoebe walks to her friend, asking, "Raven, are you okay?" Raven nods with a smile.

"Please do not say anything to anyone," Phoebe asks Raven.

The little girl hugs Phoebe while Phoebe thanks her quietly in her ear.

Phoebe comes around the corner, skipping to her mother. "Yes, Mommy."

Her mother is shaking a new lady's hand. Phoebe's mother, with dark hair and dark eyes, looks at her, introducing the new people. "This is Miss Dolores and her son. I'm sorry, what was your name again?"

Dolores replies, "His name is Joseph."

"Joseph, nice to meet you. My name is Miss Marie, and this is my daughter Phoebe. She will show you around," Marie tells him.

A young boy with dark hair and a normal tan complexion looks up, giving a partial smile as he walks away with Phoebe.

Dolores, dark hair and eyes, takes a deep breath, trying to understand her son. She turns to Marie. "I apologize for Joseph. It has not been easy for him. After his father dead in the war, the whole town turned against us. They would tell me that a boy needs a man around. They started say things about Joseph."

Marie smiles at Dolores, "That is why we are all here. We

help each other and survive. Please let me show you to your home."

Joseph sits back on a tree, watching all the kids play.

After a few months Joseph is still sitting back, watching the other children play. However, he is playing closer attention to Phoebe.

Phoebe walks over to him, asking, "Why don't you play with us?"

Joseph looks up at her, making eye contact. "I have a hard time around people."

Phoebe, crossing her arms, says, "What do you mean?"

Still looking into her eyes, he says, "I do not know. I burn things sometimes, but I am not allowed to talk about it."

Phoebe, unsure what he means, takes a chance, grabbing his hand, "You're not burning me."

Joseph smiles, getting help from her to stand up. After that day they were together all the time.

Some years later, Joseph and Phoebe are still together, doing chores, helping each other's mothers. There was never a day when you saw them apart. One day Phoebe was on the top part of the mountain, climbing a large tree. The tree stood almost two hundred feet tall. She got herself to the very top.

Phoebe is looking at the world (in her eyes), telling Joseph, "You need to see this."

Joseph replies, "You know I can't. I am too scared of heights. Please be careful I do not want you to fall."

Phoebe starts bouncing on the branch. "The branch is strong. You worry too much."

Joseph turns his head in fear. He places his hands on the tree, looking straight up at Phoebe. The tree lights on fire with Joseph now petrified for Phoebe. He screams, "Phoebe, get down. The tree is on fire."

Phoebe looks down to see a fire rising fast and starts to panic as there is no way down. Phoebe, still standing on the branch, slips off, catching herself with only her hands.

Joseph, in fear for Phoebe, screams out for help while Phoebe is hanging on the branch, screaming in a panic for her own life. Raven and their mothers arrive to see the incident.

"What happened?" Marie asks.

"I do not know. I looked up the tree, and a fire started," Joseph tells her.

"Did you touch the tree?" Dolores asks.

"Yes," Joseph replies.

With all the screaming and shaking, the branch starts to break. The flames are almost to Phoebe when she slips. Everyone below has their hearts stop. As Phoebe is falling, she closes her eyes, wishing she could fly. Then out of nowhere Phoebe turns into a red bird, catching the wind under her wings as she glides down. When she is almost to the ground, Phoebe turns back into the young girl once more, rolling in the dirt.

Phoebe, standing up, fixing her dress, rushes to Joseph, hugging him.

"Are you okay?" Joseph asks.

"Yes, I am now," Phoebe replies.

Marie also rushes in to hug her. "You need to be more careful," Marie shouts.

"I know, I am sorry," Joseph and Phoebe reply.

Marie looks at Joseph, saying, "I was talking to Phoebe."

"Oh, sorry," Joseph tells her.

Everyone proceeds to walk back to their homes when Joseph asks, "Why did you not tell me you could do that?"

Phoebe turns to him, replying, "I did not know I could." He puts his arm around her, walking back home.

Sometime later Phoebe and Joseph are getting very close, to the point where Joseph wants to ask Phoebe to marry him. Joseph plans the whole night out and is ready to ask. Joseph and Phoebe go from a walk up the mountainside toward the top. Phoebe places a blanket down so that can enjoy a picnic. They are both sitting on the blanket, looking at the stars in the same place where the tree had burned down.

"The stars look so lovely tonight," Phoebe says.

"Yes, they really do," Joseph says while pulling out the ring his mother gave him.

Phoebe feels him moving around a lot. "Are you okay, Joseph?" Joseph, who is almost ready, responds, "Yes, I am sorry. I have a rock under me. I am just trying to move it."

Phoebe turns toward him. "May I help you?"

"NO! I am sorry, no, I got it," Joseph says, feeling bad for how he spoke. Joseph turns to Phoebe, kneeling next to her. He takes a deep breath. "We have known each other for a very long time. When I first came here, you pushed me to stand. Every time I fell, you were there to catch me. You are my best friend. With all I have said, I find myself loving you."

"I love you too," Phoebe tells him.

Joseph reveals the ring. "Phoebe, will you marry me?"

Phoebe covers her face with her hands, responding, "Yes, I will." Joseph puts the ring on her hand, followed by hugging and kissing.

Sometime later Phoebe and Raven are talking about how she should not marry Joseph.

"There is something off about him," Raven tells Phoebe.

"Like what, he has been perfect to me," Phoebe tells her.

Raven point to a pile of dead animals. "What about all the animals he kills?"

"You mean the food he brings us," Phoebe tells her.

Raven takes her hand. "You know I love you. All I want is for you to be happy. You and I both know I can feel evil."

Phoebe thinks about what she is saying. "I understand what

you are saying. We are all leaving soon to a safe place for our kind. If he is evil, this place will tell us."

Raven looks Phoebe in the eyes. "All right, I pray you're right."

Phoebe starts walking toward Joseph's home to see if he is ready yet. She can hear him out back. She walks around the corner to find his back turned and he is with a small deer. Joseph has his hands on the deer.

"Hello, little fella. Are you lost? You came to the wrong place."

Joseph's hands turn into straight fire while he has the deer.

Phoebe can't see his face, but it is clear he is enjoying what he doing.

Phoebe, feeling disgusted, shouts, "What are you doing?"

Joseph stands up. "Phoebe, what are you doing here?"

"It does not matter what I am doing here. What are you doing to that poor deer?" Phoebe asks.

Joseph looks at it, saying, "I am making sure we have food."

"No, you are killing it. Enjoying it while you do it," Phoebe says, still yelling.

Raven runs over to help. "What is happening?"

Phoebe looks at Raven, saying, "You were right about him."

Joseph walks over to Raven, asking, "What did you say about me?"

Raven tells him, "I said there is something off about you."

Looking at that, now we know what. Phoebe, let's go."

Raven grabs Phoebe's hand, trying to leave, when Joseph grabs her hand.

"You are not going anywhere." Joseph's eyes turn black.

Raven screams, "Let go of me. You're burning me."

Joseph, enraged, burns even hotter, incinerating Raven in seconds. Phoebe jump back, trying not to get burned as well.

Joseph, seeing what has done, feels good about it until he

looks at Phoebe's face. When he realizes what he did, he tries to apologize. Phoebe gives him a disgusted look, running away. The other people join her. One the ladies with her tell all to join hands. Phoebe looks back at Joseph with tears in her eyes. Seconds later, everyone vanishes.

Joseph, very emotional, screams out. He walks to the middle of the small community they have made throughout the years. He looks around at everything left there, including some people.

Joseph draws a symbol in the air with his finger, saying, "This symbol will be put on the back of anyone's neck who kills for my people." The symbol starts to burn in the air.

Dolores steps out of her home, saying, "Joseph, you do not need to hurt anyone. Please calm down, son."

Joseph turns to her, saying, "It is already done. You just do not know it yet." Joseph then turns his whole body into a fire, burning everything within fifty yards.

Phoebe and company appear on an island. Phoebe starts putting up a protective bubble. "Only those who are good shall enter. No evil of any kind enters this land without alarms sounding. This place with be for my people and people like us."

They proceed to build homes and plant crops. Phoebe can't stop thinking about what happened. Her heart and her mind feel broken apart. Love is there, but the anger is too. Feeling confused, she pushes to get everything built, never to talk about it again.

James looks around to find that he just ran into Phoebe.

"I am so sorry. May I call you Grandma?" James asks.

Phoebe looks into James eyes with a straight face. "If you want to. I am your great-grandmother after all."

James continues walking home. James gets home, walking straight into his room. Lying on his bed, he begins to think about everything he saw moments ago. There is a lot of things no one knows about. With everything on his mind, James falls asleep.

The next morning James is woken up by Rae, who is knocking and shouting on his front door.

"James, I know you're here. Please answer, James."

James jumps out of bed, still ever upset. Power walking through the house.

James grabs the door, opening it with authority, "WHAT?" Rae steps back, saying, "I'm sorry, I wanted to let you know I found a way."

James's mind only points to one thing when he asks, "Are you saying what I think you're saying?"

Rae smiles. "Yes, I found a way to get to the other plane."

James also begins smiling while asking, "How? What do I need to do?" James invites Rae into the house.

Rae sits down, telling James, "I was looking at how everything works. I started thinking about your grandfather and the way he moves throughout planes. I think because you share his bloodline you might be able to do so as well. All we need is a way to open it." *Knock, knock.* James turns his head back to the door. He stands up to open the door. James finds Miss Star standing there, asking, "May I come in? We need to talk."

James, with a deep breath, asks, "Do I have a choice? You run this place."

Miss Star, feeling hurt by that comment, says, "You always have a choice."

James lets her in to talk.

Miss Star notices Rae already inside and asks, "What is going on here?"

Rae looks up, saying, "Hello, Miss Star, I'm helping James with a problem he was having."

"May I ask what the problem is?" Miss Star asks.

Rae looks at James and Miss Star, feeling the tension in the air. She responds slowly, "He asked me about other planes."

Miss Star, with a look of frustration, tells James, "I thought we said that was impossible."

James looks at her, saying, "Not anymore. You see Rae thinks because Joseph can do it and I'm part of his bloodline, I might be able as well."

Miss Star looks at Rae, asking, "Is this true?"

"Theoretically, yes. It is very possible," Rae responds.

"Okay, when do we leave?" Miss Star asks.

James steps in. "Wait, no one said anything about you going. You are the one who said it not safe."

"I'm not letting you go by yourself," Miss Star tells James.

James looks at Rae, saying, "Please tell her it is not possible."

Rae thinks about it, then says, "I think I might be able to make it possible. I would need some of your blood, and as long as she has in with her, it could help her be safe."

Miss Star looks at James. "There, it's settled. I will be going with you."

Rae stands up, saying, "There is still one thing we need to do for this to work."

James looks her way, saying, "The way into the plane."

Miss Star looks at both of them, saying, "I know how we can do that."

James asks, "How did you learn that?"

Miss Star looks at him as she sits down, saying, "My sister, your mother, she wanted to do that same thing. Your father, being my guardian, wouldn't let me go with her without him. We found out everything we needed to know from Eugene. Shame he is no longer around."

James smiles. "He never left."

Miss Star remembers James talking about seeing him.

Rae asks them both, "When did we want to go?"

James is quick to respond, "As soon as we can."

Rae stands up, saying, "Okay, I'll get to work on it." Rae leaves the house, heading home to work on everyone being safe.

Miss Star stays to talk to James. "Are you sure this is what you want to do?" Miss Star asks.

James looks her in the eyes. "More than anything. To know that my mother is trapped somewhere, I might be able to fix it. Whether she goes to heaven or whatever could happen, just knowing I helped her like she did with me—that is all I want."

Miss Star nods her head with a smile on her face and hugs him. As Miss Star is leaving, David shows up.

"Hey, James, what is going on? Everything okay?" David asks.

"Yeah, everything is great," James replies.

David notices the smile on James's face and asks, "You seem to be in a good mood."

"I am. Things are finally going my way," James tells David.

David sits closer to James. "What do you mean?"

James turns to him, saying, "Well, we found a way to go to the spiritual plane where my mother is. Aunt Estrella is going to help me make things right."

David turns speechless as James tells him, "I'm going to bed. Good night."

David jumps up. "No, I won't let you go. It's too dangerous."

James walks to him with a smile. "David, I'm all grown up. You can't tell me no."

"Then you're grounded," David says to him.

James, still with a smile, says, "Nice try. You can't ground me either."

David, feeling desperate, shouts, "Then I'm going too."

James walks out of his room, this time without a smile. "Okay, I'll let you know when we are ready."

David sits down with only one thing on his mind, *What the hell did I just do?*

Miss Star gets back home to find Phoebe standing at the doorway like she knows something is about to happen.

Miss Star stops in her tracks. "Hi, how is your night?"

"Everything was great until I had a feeling you were about to do something stupid," Phoebe tells her.

Miss Star gives her a look of confusion, "What do you mean?"

Phoebe gives her death stare. "Estrella, do not try to lie to me. What are you about to do?"

Miss Star tries to make Phoebe understand by saying, "We know how to save Marcelina." Miss Star can see Phoebe is trying to hide the happy/sad feeling on her face.

"It does not matter. It is too dangerous."

"I'm sorry to tell you, but you cannot stop this. I have a chance to help my sister, your granddaughter, I am taking it. I love you very much, but I need to do this," Miss Star tells her as she gathers everything she might need.

Miss Star walks up to Phoebe, kissing her on the cheek, as if it was the last time, she might see her.

Phoebe stands in the same place, thinking about everything that could happen. Phoebe sits down, knowing there is nothing she can do to stop the event from happening. Phoebe starts to cry, knowing what will happen. Miss Star is walking back to James's home when she runs into Benjamin.

Benjamin walks up to her, saying, "NOPE, not without me."

"You are not going," Miss Star tells him.

Benjamin smiles. "You are not going to the spirit plane, where my wife is, without me."

"Fine, then tell your son the same thing. He is the one that is trying," Miss Star tells him.

"I will. I just got him back. I'm not going to lose him again," Benjamin replies.

They both walk to James's home. James is at home getting ready when AJ shows up spontaneously.

"Hey, James, I'm ready," AJ tells James.

James, packing things in his bag, asks, "For what?"

AJ put a hand on his shoulder, saying, "You really thought I was going to let you go without me?"

James turns his head, looking at AJ, saying, "I was just making sure."

Mari walks into the room as well. "I have everything I need."

James looks at her, saying, "HELL, NO. I cannot let you go."

"What do you mean, no? You cannot tell me what to do," Mari tells James.

"I'm not trying to tell you what to do. I cannot lose you. You mean too much to me," James tells her.

Mari looks him in the eyes, saying, "You mean the same to me. You think I can lose you. I need to know you're okay."

James smiles, turning to see if there is anything else, he might need.

CHAPTER 12

IT'S TIME

The next morning everyone is at James's home waiting for Rae. James is feeling scared, realizing what is about to happen. Everyone is thinking about what they are getting into, feeling the same. *Knock, knock.*

Everyone's heart stop for a second, knowing it's time. James opens the door, inviting Rae in. Rae walks in, looking around at the room full of people. In the room is Benjamin, Bob, David, Miss Star, AJ, and Mari.

Rae, seeing everyone, says, "I had a feeling."

Everyone looks around when AJ says, "We are a close family."

Rae takes out several vials, saying, "I have everything we need mixed up in these. Th ere is only one thing we need for it to work, your blood."

Benjamin stands up quick. "Why his blood? Use mine, I am his son."

Rae looks at him, saying, "No, it needs to be James. He is a firestarter.

Plus, more likely to him because of everything he can see." James lifts his arm, saying, "Take what you need."

Rae begins taking blood from James. She looks at Benjamin, saying, "I don't think you need this potion. You have his blood in you, so you should be pass through unharmed."

"Are you sure?" Benjamin asks.

"Yes, like I said, James is like him, so we need his help to pass through," Rae tells him.

Rae has the blood, adding it to the potion. Mari notices there are five vials and wonders how it works.

Rae places her hands above the group of vials, saying, "Okay, they are ready. You will need to drink this. They might feel like drinking hot sauce."

First, AJ walks up, taking the vial like a shot, saying in a harsh voice, "Smooth."

He is followed by Mari, then David, and finally Miss Star.

Miss Star asks, "Is there anything else that we need to do?"

"No, that is it. Let's go."

Mari looks at Rae, asking, "You have one left. You need to take the last one."

Benjamin and Bob look at Rae. Everyone else looks at Rae as well.

Rae looks at them, saying, "I don't need to. I found out a

while ago that Benjamin and Bob are my uncles. My father was their brother."

Miss Star walks up to Rae. "I remember your father, but he never told me."

Rae looks at her, saying, "It's okay, we have a job to do. Let's go get this done."

They proceed to Eugene, hoping he can help them get into the spiritual plane. James can see him walking straight to him.

"Hello, sir, how are you doing this morning?" James greets him.

"I am doing very well, young man. Thank you for asking," Eugene responds.

"I have a question for you, sir," James tells him.

Eugene smiles at him. "You would like to know about the spiritual plane."

James smiles back. "Something like that. I would like to go to the spiritual plane."

Eugene looks James in the eyes, saying, "Do you understand the dangers behind this?"

"Yes, sir, I do," James responds.

"You have already made yourself ready to be there," Eugene tells them.

"Yes, sir," James responds.

"Okay, I will help you. Be careful," Eugene tells them.

"Yes, sir," James responds.

To everyone else Eugene makes himself seen. Everyone is nervous with what they are seeing.

Eugene tells them, "Going into this place is extremely dangerous. There are things that will try to kill you. Things you couldn't imagine. Stay together at all times. I hope what you are looking for is easy to find."

Eugene begins moving his right hand in a circle over and over, moving faster and faster until a portal opens. "Make sure you find what you want. Otherwise, you will not be able to come back. One more thing, do not die there. You will never be able to rest. Your soul will be trapped forever."

They start to walk into the portal. Eugene stops James, saying, "You will not need your bags. Nothing there will be harmed by anything in them. You can only use your gifts. If you don't have powers, you don't fight. I pray you won't need to. Good luck to all of you."

One by one they each step through the portal.

AJ bends down, trying to catch his breath. "Oh man, is this what you felt like in your first teleport, James?"

James, not taking his eyes out the goal, responds, "Something like that, just breathe. You'll be fine."

They all start walking forward. Everything they see looks like a dry desert. The sky is dark with more reddish clouds with lightning. There are no trees, no anything, only pure death. As they continue walking, it looks as though they are walking up a hill. The only sound you can hear is the lightning crashing.

They walk a little further, making it over the hill. James can see someone standing there at the bottom. The person has long hair, looking like what he saw of his mother.

James runs to the person, shouting, "MOM, I'm coming."

Everyone watches James run, shouting, and tries to stop him.

James makes it to the person, placing his hand on her shoulder, saying, "I found you."

The person vanishes, like the wind blowing away a sand statue.

Everyone rushes to James with Benjamin asking, "What were you doing?"

"I thought I saw…I thought that was my mother," James replies.

Benjamin puts his hands-on James's face, looking his in the eyes, "I understand that, but you need to stay with us. We have no idea what is in here."

James nods, understanding what he is being told.

They keep walking forward, looking everyway there is. After sometime Mari can see something ahead and calls everyone together. They are looking at what looks to be someone sitting by what could be a dead tree reading a book.

"Is that real?" AJ asks.

"I have no idea," Mari responds.

"That looks like…" James says.

"I know, but together," Benjamin tells him.

James gives a look, saying, "I know that."

Miss Star steps in, asking, "Are we going down there or standing here? I personally would like to go down there."

They all slowly begin walking down looking at this person sitting there. Without meaning to, James shouts, "MOM."

The person looks up and shouts, "Who…wait, James? Is that my baby James?" She stands up, rushing over to him.

James runs to her, picking her up with the largest hug on his life and tears in his eyes. While hugging her, James says, "Mom, I found you. I knew you were here."

Marcelina looks at him. "How are you here?"

Benjamin walks up to her, unsure what will happen. She turns him around in a circle checking his neck, then gives him the same hug as James. "I missed you so much, my love."

Benjamin, with tears in eyes, responds, "I missed you. I love you so much."

Miss Star steps in also with tears. "Get over here, sis," she says, hugging Marcelina as tight as she can.

David is standing back because he feels like he failed her.

Marcelina looks at him. "What are you doing over there?"

David tells her, "I failed you. You're here."

Marcelina opens her arms, saying, "No, you didn't. My son is alive.

You saved him like I asked. Now come here."

David starts to cry, walking to her, hugging her as well.

After all hugs are finished, Marcelina looks around at everyone and asks, "As much as I'm so happy to see everyone. What are you all doing here?"

James tells her, "I saw you coming through to our world asking for help. We are here to help you."

Marcelina looks at her son, "You saw me?" She looks at everyone else. "My son saw me?"

James grabs her arm, responding, "Yes, Mom. Now let's go."

Marcelina pulls back. "That's not what I need your help with. There is a creature here that eats souls."

James tells her, "No problem. I am very strong."

Marcelina, looking impressed, asks, "Really, what is your gift?" James smiles, saying, "According to Aunt Estrella, the most powerful firestarter she ever saw."

Marcelina face has fear written all over it.

Miss Star steps in, saying, "Marcelina, don't worry. Not like that.

He only cares about helping other people like you."

Marcelina looks back at her, asking, "Are you sure, Estrella?"

Miss Star smiles. "I promise."

Marcelina look back at James. "Okay, as long as you keep it good.

I'm happy."

"I promise, Mom," James tells her.

"Now what is this thing you are scared of, Mom?" James asks.

Marcelina can see it. She tells everyone to duck, pointing to it. A 160-foot demon-like creature with wings and octopus-arms-like face touching the ground, sucking up souls like a tornado.

Marcelina tells them, "They call it the Soul Eater."

James's face says it all, turning white and pale.

Marcelina looks at his, asking, "James, are you okay?"

James shakes his face, bringing color back to it. "Yes, I'm fine. It's bigger than I thought. I can take care of it."

Marcelina grabs him, saying, "No, don't burn it."

James looks back at her and asks, "Why?"

She quickly says, "I just don't want you hurting yourself doing that. You will need to get close. That's too dangerous."

James responds, "Okay. Mari, can you freeze it?" "I can try," Mari responds.

"I think we can all help her take it down," James says to everyone.

They all get moving, but Marcelina grabs James. "Please don't leave me alone."

James looks at her. "Okay, I'll stay."

Miss Star looks back at them. "James, will you be okay?"

"Yes, I'll be fine," James responds.

They all are getting closer to the Soul Eater that don't even looked like it is looking toward them. It is more like moving away from them. Marcelina moves her hand, motioning toward them. The Soul Eater turns its head toward everyone. It turns back, now moving to them.

James looks at Marcelina, asking, "What are you doing?"

She looks at him in a demonic voice, "Making sure my baby eats." AJ, feeling James, tells everyone to go back. Marcelina quickly turns into Joseph.

James backs up really fast. "What? I thought you were dead."

"Where do you think you are? Perfect place to meet again. When I saw you were here, I had to play that role. I knew I could get you to do anything as her," Joseph tells him.

James stands up, asking, "What did you do with her?"

Joseph looks at him, laughing. "I have been here for a long time. I killed her over and over. Then, after I was bored with it, I fed her to my Soul Eater. The more it eats, the stronger I get."

James looks around, then says, "I have one question I have been dying to know."

"Yes, what is it?" Joseph asks.

James starts standing. "Does cold burn you too?"

Joseph's face turns confused as he says, "What?"

Then Mari hits him with ice balls she made, allowing James to get away. James runs as fast as can, catching up to everyone else. Joseph looks back to see where they ran to, shouting out and moving his hand, commanding the Soul Eater to go after them.

David turns around and shouts, "The Soul Eater is on our tail."

Unsure where they can run, James stops in his tracks. "I have an idea."

Benjamin runs to him, saying, "You do not need to do this."

James looks back, saying, "There is nowhere for us to run. I think I might be able to stop or hurt it."

"Then I'm not leaving," Benjamin tells him.

James looks at him. "Dad, you are not a firestarter. You will get hurt if you are too close."

Benjamin looks at James, knowing he is right. He walks away.

Mari runs up to James. "Let me help."

Mari and James take each other's hands to use their gift together. The Soul Eater is within fifty yards of them, moving slowly. Mari and James lift both their hands into the air, firing the fire/ice mix they used to destroy Joseph. The Soul Eater is getting hit with the blast and tries to defend itself with its hands. Mari and James are pushing the blast as hard as they can, destroying a wing and part of its face until they get hit by a hand of the creature, sending them flying.

Miss Star tries to use her flying to distract it while Benjamin lifts the ground around it, pulling it into the ground. Bob walk up to the Soul Eater's body, giving a whistle sound. The sound turns into a high frequency force that starts to rip off more of the face and the other wing of the Soul Eater.

AJ rushes to check on James and Mari. They both rise to their feet, watching everyone else fighting. However, Rae is standing back with her eyes closed and arms out to the side. James looks at her, thinking, *what's she doing?* The Soul Eater reaches out with its suction arms from its face, trying to grab Rae. Rae's body lifts off the ground. She opens her eyes glowing light purple. A purple ball of light forms in the palms of her hands. At this moment the Soul Eater is pulling itself out of ground. Rae claps her hands together, causing a shockwave echoing throughout the sky, hitting the Soul Eater hard. She claps two more times until the Soul Eater falls backward, hitting the ground hard. Everyone comes together ready for whatever might happen next.

Joseph, nowhere to be found, speaks, "Do you really think you have won anything yet? In this world, I am a god."

Benjamin replies, "If you are such a god, why are you hiding?"

Joseph lets out a big laugh. "You think I am hiding. You really are dumber than Bob. I am everywhere. I see all." James steps to the Soul Eater.

"If you are so powerful, then tell me why your creature is down." Joseph reappears, levitating twenty feet above them. "It's not down, regenerating takes time."

James walks away from everyone, taunting Joseph. "You do know that I'm not scared of some three-hundred-year-old. I already stopped you once."

Joseph looks at him, saying, "You're right. That's why I don't need to do anything."

The Soul Eater's hand slaps down on James, leaving a massive crater in the ground. Everyone stands, still in disbelief, not a sound.

Joseph, feeling good about what he did, looks to the rest. "You will bow to me or suffer the same fate."

The hand lifts up with James bent down, on guard himself. Standing above him with a force field blocking all contact is Marcelina.

Joseph looks down, seeing her, saying, "NO, he was mine."

James, realizing what happened, can't take his eyes off her.

Marcelina, helping him up, responds, "Joseph, I keep telling you to stop trying. You will never get rid of me. You went after my son. That makes my very mad."

James is still looking at her, still in shock.

Marcelina walks over to her family with James and says, "Leave my family alone."

Joseph shoots a stream of fire at her.

James cries out, "MOM."

Joseph stops the fire with Marcelina, and she is still standing there.

James asks, "How?"

Marcelina looks at her son, saying, "My grandmother is a phoenix. I happen to be fireproof. Plus, someone had to hold you when you lit yourself up as a baby."

James smiles with a small laugh.

Joseph lowers himself to the ground, asking, "Do you all really think you can stop me?"

Then a voice shouts, "NO."

Everyone looks to see Phoebe walking to them.

Phoebe looks at Joseph, asking, "What happened to you?"

Joseph looks at a girl he knew once upon a time. "How are you alive? I hit you with the death spell. My own creation. No one survives that."

Phoebe tells Joseph, "How could you forget? I am a Phoenix. I can never die forever. I will always come back."

Joseph slowly walks to her. "I am so glad it didn't work."

Phoebe places her hand on his face. "You know I never stopped loving you."

Joseph, feeling love again, says, "I never stopped loving you either. You were my everything."

"What happened? You were the most amazing person I ever met," Phoebe tells him.

Joseph looks down. "When you left, you took my heart with you."

Phoebe places both hands on his face and says, "I have been wanting to give you something for a long time."

Phoebe lifts into the air, completely on fire, like a phoenix bird. She slams her hands together like wings, hitting Joseph with a massive fire wave, mix of wind from wings with the wind being fire, sending Joseph flying.

The Soul Eater rushes to Phoebe. Phoebe hits it the same way as Joseph. The Soul Eater flies back, hitting Mari on the way down. James rushes to Mari, holding her in his arms. He looks around, feeling like he is in a dream.

Marcelina screams out, "JAMES."

A stream of fire starts coming from James, burning in a ring around him and Mari. Something that was always fuzzy is now happening. James thinks about the prophecy. *Is it this world that burns as it stands?*

Miss Star screams for help. The fire ring lifts up and expands out more. James places his hand on Mari's heart to feel for beating.

James grabs both charms, holding them tight in his own hand. Both charms start to glow. James, with her leaning against his body, she uses it to hit the Soul Eater. With the blast from James and Mari, the Soul Eater explodes.

Joseph screams out, "NOOOO." Mari opens her eyes.

James looks at her, asking, "Are you okay?"

"I think so," Mari responds.

James helps to her to her feet. James looks at Joseph, saying, "I am done with all these games."

Joseph looks back at him, saying, "So am I. AQHA DEATH TONL."

A green light flies past James, hitting Phoebe. Everyone but James rushes to her. Phoebe's body burns into a pile of ash. James, who just watched his great-grandmother die, is now extremely pissed. Still having both charms in his hand, the charms begin to glow even brighter this time. James's eyes turn black, then change to a solid blue.

James, who isn't even heating up, looks at Joseph, "You have almost killed the woman I love, my mother again, and now you killed my grandmother in front of me. Please allow me to repay the favor."

James lifts arm, burning this world he is in. Then James hears his mother say, "James, you need to relax."

With a wave of his hand, everyone is back in the living world on the island. James, who is still on the spiritual plane starts fighting Joseph. Joseph hitting him with everything he has, either magic or otherwise.

Joseph finds an opening and screams out, "AQHA DEATH TONL," hitting James dead on.

James takes the hit like he only got a small push.

Joseph can't believe what he just saw and realizes what is happening.

James can see it too, saying, "I guess I found it."

Joseph, in shock, says, "Not possible."

James looks at him and says, "I FOUND MEMPA."

Joseph tries hitting him again with fire and his death spell at the same time. At the same moment, James drops his hands to the ground, lighting up the hottest blue flame everywhere. A fire so hot that the world is burning down as it stands. James, seeing everything burn, can still see Joseph. He keeps pushing the heat hotter and hotter. Then a cold flame comes through the fire, grabbing Joseph, pulling him down.

Joseph, stuck in the cold flame, can't move, and his body melts down, bones and all.

James can see there is nothing left but a world completely destroyed. James takes a step like he is walking out of a room, stepping back into the living world. James can see everyone again. He run to everyone with a smile, asking, "You all made it out. Where's Mom?"

Benjamin puts his arm around James. "Your mother has been dead for a long time. I don't think she would have come back with us."

James, feeling like he failed, hears, "Now, didn't I say you can't stop me?" James head pops up and sees his mother made it back as well.

AJ asks, "How is this possible?"

Marcelina tells him, "They say MEMPA is so powerful it can bring back the dead."

James, realizing they lost Phoebe, says, "Mom, I'm so sorry. I couldn't save Grandma."

"I wouldn't say that," Miss Star walks to James holding a baby.

James looks at the baby, saying, "You mean to say that this is Phoebe?"

Miss Star smiles, "Yes, you cannot kill her. She is reborn every time."

James looks around, taking a head count. "Okay, we have everyone here," James says with relief.

"What happened to Joseph?" Bob asks.

James, slow to respond, says, "Like the prophecy said, a child born from good and evil with burn down the world as it stands. The world took Joseph with it."

Benjamin asks, "How did you do it all?"

James responds, "I found MEMPA. That's all anyone needs to know."

James looks at his hands and sees the marks from the charms now on his palms.

"I only need to know one thing," Miss Star tells James.

"Anything," James replies.

Miss Star asks, "You got your mother. Joseph is gone. Are we done yet? Are we safe?"

James walks to her, placing his left hand on her shoulder, "Done for now. Safe, forever and always."

James smiles, shouting, "WE ARE NOW FREE. Enjoy your life. Live, love, and know we are here for anything you might need."

The community cheers out in happiness. James and Mari kiss during the celebration.

After a few days everything seems to be perfect. Yet James feels like something is off.

On the spiritual plane everything has been burned down. The Soul Eater is a large pile of rock and dust. Around this dark place something is walking around. A man walks by Joseph's body pile. The man looks around, trying to find any life left. With nothing found, he sits by him, enjoying the fact that he is dead. He is laughing and taunting him for trying to take his soul. The man puts his face right up to the middle of the pile and screams, laughing, when a hand grabs him by the throat.

To be continued

I dedicate this book to my amazing family. To whom I would not have the courage to have followed my dreams. To my children Aiden, Miyah, Nuvia, and Phoenix, there is nothing you can't do if you put your heart into it and always give it your all. To my incredible wife Marivel, thank you for believing in me the way you have and continue to do so. You are the best half of me and I am the luckiest man to have you. I love you all from the bottom of my heart.

www.ingramcontent.com/pod-product-compliance
Lightning Source LLC
LaVergne TN
LVHW091548060526
838200LV00036B/749